INVERCLYDE LIBRARIES

This edition published in 2018 by Pokey Hat

Pokey Hat is an imprint of Cranachan Publishing Limited

First published in 2015 by Cargo Publishing

ISBN: 978-1-911279-29-7
eISBN: 978-1-911279-30-3

Cover design based on an illustration by Qynn Herd

Cover photographs
© shutterstock.com / Niko28 / ssuaphotos / TroobaDoor

www.cranachanpublishing.co.uk

@cranachanbooks

cranachan

PRAISE FOR

THE
WRECK
OF THE
ARGYLL

'THE BOOK IS A THRILLING AND FASCINATING STORY BASED ON
AN ACTUAL EXCITING EVENT.'
Theresa Breslin, Carnegie Medal-winning author of
Whispers in the Graveyard.

'IT'S AN EXCITING AND FAST-PACED SPY THRILLER. THE
WRECK OF THE ARGYLL IS MY KIND OF STORY.'
Allan Burnett, author and historian.

'PERFECTLY CAPTURES THE CLANDESTINE WORLD OF SPIES
AND ALL THE EXCITEMENT AND DANGER LURKING THERE.'
Abi Elphinstone, author of The Dreamsnatcher.

'THE PERFECT MIX OF BRAVE CHILDREN, DASTARDLY VILLAINS
AND A TOTALLY DRAMATIC BUT BELIEVABLE PLOT.'
Jo Clarke, children's librarian
(bookloverjo.wordpress.com).

'FAST-PACED WITH SOME GREAT DIALOGUE EXCHANGES AND THERE'S THE MOST FANTASTIC CONCLUSION... IT REALLY IS QUITE A LITTLE GEM.'
Wendy at Little Bookness Lane
(littlebooknesslane.wordpress.com).

'THIS BOOK IS BRILLIANT, I READ IT IN ONE SITTING... LOVED THE DESCRIPTIONS AND THE TENSION!'
Fiona Sharp
(independentbookreviews.co.uk).

'THE STORY IS ACTION-PACKED, FAST-PACED, AND EASY TO FOLLOW, MAKING IT IDEAL FOR MIDDLE-GRADE READERS.'
Sonia Alejandra Rodriguez, at the American Library
Association's Booklist Online.

'SUSPENSE SLOWLY BUILDS AS NANCY PURSUES HER THEORY, AND THE PACING REACHES A FEVER PITCH AS HER SUSPICIONS BECOME CONFIRMED... A SATISFYING WORLD WAR I MYSTERY WITH AGE-APPROPRIATE THEMES THAT WILL RESONATE WITH YOUNG READERS.'
Julie Shatterly, at the School Library Journal.

To Sandra, for everything

CHAPTER ONE
DUNDEE

Nancy kept to the shadows as she followed the spy. She'd trailed him from his big house on Perth Road all the way down the Nethergate, his long strides making it difficult for her to keep up. Her chest ached in the cold October air as she panted for breath, and she could feel the strain in her calves. She'd been trying to follow him every evening for a whole week, but tonight was the first time she'd managed to keep up with him all the way into the centre of town. She *had* to find out what he was up to. What reason did a school teacher have to be sneaking about the streets after dark—particularly when there was a war on?

As the spy neared the corner he slowed down, and Nancy ducked into the doorway of a boot shop just in time. The man looked around then pulled the brim of his hat down and turned onto Union Street.

Nancy's heart was beating in her chest like a snare drum. What if he'd seen her? She had no excuse for being out in the street this late. A twelve-year-old girl from a reasonably respectable family had no reason to be out and about in the centre of Dundee at eleven o'clock at night. She was small and skinny with a pointed nose and shoulder-length mousy-brown hair, not much different from any other Dundonian girl her age, but looking nondescript wouldn't be any protection when she was the only girl on the street. She closed her eyes and tried to breathe slowly. Eventually her heartbeat calmed, and she risked a peek.

There was no-one in sight. She trotted carefully to the corner, then looked down Union Street. In the waning moonlight, visible through the sparse clouds, she could see all the way down the steep street to the silvery ribbon of the River Tay in the distance, but there was no sign of the man. Did she dare follow him? What if he was waiting in the shadows? Waiting to snatch her—or worse? Who knew what one of the Kaiser's spies would do to keep his cover. Maybe they'd find her body floating in the Tay. Maybe they'd never find her body at all...

Nancy took a deep breath and made her way down the street.

Every shadowed doorway held the potential for terror. She crept past each one, going so slowly that by the time she reached the end of the street, she knew that Mr. Simpson was long gone.

She stood in the street, hands on her hips, trying to

work out where he'd disappeared to. In one direction was the Tay Bridge railway station. What could a spy do there? There were troop trains, she supposed. He might be counting carriages full of soldiers. Or plotting sabotage.

In the other direction were the docks. A few years before the war started, a German spy might have kept himself busy around the Earl Grey Dock for weeks, watching and taking notes as the submarines came and went. But now, in 1915, Dundee's docks held only civilian ships. Nancy had heard people complain that Dundee wasn't important any more, and that all the navy ships and submarines were up at Scapa Flow or down at Rosyth. Merchant ships were important, but not as important as troops.

The railway station it was, then.

As she drew closer she could hear the hustle of men and machines. Ambulances and cars and trucks stood outside the station with orderlies leaning on their bonnets, smoking cigarettes and talking in low voices. In the distance came the whistle of a train, then the familiar chuff-chuff sound that had always seemed so romantic to her, a sound that spoke of adventure and far-away places. Not that she'd ever been further than Arbroath.

'Step lively, lads,' said one man in a voice that carried through the cold night air but still seemed strangely subdued, as if he'd tempered a shouted command to something more gentle and respectful. 'The train's coming in.'

The orderlies threw their cigarettes to the ground and made their way inside the station. Within minutes the first soldiers emerged, some on crutches, some bandaged, others being carried on stretchers. With quiet efficiency they were squeezed into the waiting vehicles, as many as could fit in each one.

When the first ambulance was full, the man in charge consulted a clipboard and banged on the bonnet. 'Royal Infirmary,' he said, and the ambulance drove off. As each vehicle filled up, he sent it on its way with its cargo of wounded soldiers. The worst cases—the ones on stretchers—were sent to the Royal Infirmary and the Eastern Hospital in ambulances. The walking wounded were packed into cars and delivery vans and sent to Caird Rest nursing home on the Nethergate, or Cox's School in Lochee, or all the way to The Lodge in Broughty Ferry.

Nancy hid in the shadows and counted the soldiers. Ten. Twenty. Fifty. A hundred. Exactly a hundred wounded soldiers, dispersed to all parts of Dundee for treatment.

What touched Nancy's heart was the quiet. The soldiers barely made a sound as they emerged from the station and got into the waiting vehicles. They seemed broken in spirit as well as in body.

An anger rose in Nancy's throat, and her fists clenched.

The spy could be hiding in the shadows right at that moment, just like she was, counting the wounded, only with grim satisfaction in his heart instead of the misery she felt. He'd be happy at the prospect of reporting so many casualties to his grateful master the Kaiser.

She had to stop him.

It was long past midnight, and Nancy knew there was nothing else she could do to track down Mr. Simpson the spy. It was time for her to head for home before she was missed.

Not that it was likely that anyone had noticed she was missing from her bed. Her sister Nelly was fourteen, and had left school to work in the jute factory making ropes for army tents. Her mother worked as a cleaner at the Royal Infirmary. Her father spent his nights baking, and his days teaching military cooks. When they weren't working, her family slept the sleep of people who were giving everything they had. They were all so busy and exhausted with their own efforts to help in the war that they rarely even noticed she existed.

She couldn't blame them for that. But she wanted to help out in her own way, and they'd refused to let her volunteer at the hospital or even to go to work in the jute factory. Army tents needed ropes, and if she was at least doing that, it would be something that would make her feel less useless. What was the point of learning arithmetic and handwriting when there was *real* work to be done?

She was so distracted with her thoughts that she didn't realise she'd walked right up to the Howff, the ancient cemetery in the centre of Dundee. In daylight, this would be the way she'd normally head home, but crossing a cemetery in bright sunshine was one thing. Walking through centuries-old graves after midnight, just a few nights before Hallowe'en, was quite another.

She paused at the entrance and stared up at the dark grey stone archway. In the moonlight the dragons on Dundee's coat of arms above the gate seemed to shimmer and wriggle as if alive.

No. She'd been brave enough for one night. She'd walk *around* the Howff, not through it. Her decision made, she patted the iron bars of the gate in farewell, and realised with a laugh that the cemetery gates were locked anyway. With a grin, she turned to leave, and a coarse voice came out of the shadows.

'What are you doing here?'

A rough hand grabbed at her sleeve, and she pulled away. Three lads, not much older than her, but dirty-faced and wiry and feral-looking, crowded up to her.

'This is our street,' said one. 'Pay the toll, or pay the price.'

'Please,' said Nancy. 'I'm just going home.' She backed

away from the lads.

'You shouldn't be out so late on your own,' said another. 'It's dangerous. Give us sixpence, and we'll see you home safe.' He grinned, revealing broken teeth more like a shark's than a boy's.

'There's all sorts out after midnight,' said the third. 'Dangerous types.' He pulled a small knife out of his pocket. It was more like a knife you'd use to peel an apple than threaten someone, but Nancy's blood ran cold at the sight of it.

The three lads spread out, penning her against the wall of the Howff. She clenched her fists and cursed her luck. She had no money to give them. The lads were all bigger than her, although not by much. The one with the knife, the one to her left, was the shortest, but she didn't want to risk getting cut. Of the other two, the one in the middle was tallest and toughest-looking, so that left the one on the right.

Nancy faked to the left, then drove her shoulder into the chest of the lad on the right. He fell back with an 'oof', landing hard on his bottom, and she nearly got past, nearly got away, but the tall one in the middle shouted and grabbed her wrist. She wriggled and pulled, but his grip was strong.

'Give us your money,' he snarled.

'I don't have any,' she snapped back in reply.

'Then give us your shoes,' said the lad with the knife.

'I bet I can sell them for a couple of shillings down the market.'

'I'm not giving you my shoes,' said Nancy. 'Don't be ridiculous.'

'Ooh, listen to her. Ridiculous, are we?' said the lad with the knife. 'Hold her down while I get her shoes off.'

The other two lads grabbed an arm each and pushed Nancy to the ground. As the third reached for her right foot, she kicked out and caught him on the bony point of his wrist with the sharp toe of her shoe. He squealed and dropped the knife, and it clattered into the shadows.

'You'll regret that,' he sobbed, clutching his wrist. He drew back his leg to kick Nancy, then suddenly pitched forward and crumpled to the pavement.

'You're the one who's going to regret coming onto my patch,' growled the boy who'd knocked the lad to the ground. He was no older or taller than the lads who'd attacked Nancy, maybe thirteen at most, and his skinny frame showed through his threadbare clothes, but even in the moonlight Nancy could see a fierceness in his eyes and in the set of his jaw. His dark hair fell in an untidy uncut wave across his pale face and a smudge of dirt darkened his cheek.

The tallest of the lads leapt up and swung at the newcomer, who took the punch on his shoulder without flinching then headbutted the lad right on the nose.

Nancy climbed to her feet and stood shoulder to

shoulder with the boy. She had no idea who he was, but right at that moment he was the best friend she'd ever had.

The three lads gathered themselves and faced the pair. 'Jamie the Howff,' spat the tallest lad. 'You filthy, stinking, rat-faced tinker.'

'Get out of here,' said Jamie. 'Go home. Go and bully your little sisters or something.'

The lad who'd had the knife spat on the ground, then, warily, the three made their way down the street, glancing back to make sure Jamie wasn't following them.

'Are you all right?' asked Jamie.

Nancy nodded.

'What are you doing out here at this time of night?'

'None of your business,' said Nancy.

'That's a fine attitude to show for someone who's just saved your life,' said Jamie.

'Or saved my shoes, at any rate,' said Nancy, and they both laughed. 'I'm sorry. I was being rude. Can we start again?'

Jamie insisted on walking Nancy home. They trod silently along the deserted streets. Nancy noticed that Jamie's eyes were constantly looking around, as if he expected to be set upon at any moment. There was a strange look to his face, at once hunted and predatory.

'So, you're Jamie the Howff,' she began.

'Don't,' said Jamie. 'My name's Jamie Balfour.'

'Why do they call you Jamie the Howff?'

Jamie was silent for a moment. 'Because I live in the cemetery,' he said quietly.

'Don't you have a home? A mother and father?'

Jamie shook his head. 'My pa's gone. My ma wasn't interested in anything but gin and giving me the belt, so I left home.'

'That's awful,' said Nancy. 'But you can't live in the cemetery. What happens when it rains? When it snows?'

Jamie shrugged. 'The Howff's warm enough. They say the vapours from the corpses rise up through the ground to give it its balmy atmosphere.'

Nancy shuddered. 'Don't say such things,' she said.

Jamie laughed.

'How do you eat?' asked Nancy.

'I get by.'

Nancy glanced at how skinny he was and shook her head. 'I'll bring you some food.'

'I don't need it,' said Jamie.

'To say thank you,' said Nancy. 'For saving my shoes. It's the least I can do.'

They walked in silence for a while.

'I'm forgetting my manners,' said Nancy. 'I'm Nancy Caird.'

'And what are you doing out this late at night, Nancy Caird?'

'Important work,' said Nancy. 'For the war effort.'

Jamie laughed.

'Don't laugh,' snapped Nancy. 'It's true!'

'Oh aye,' said Jamie. 'I'm sure.'

'It is!' Nancy almost stamped her foot in frustration. She stopped in her tracks. Jamie looked at her, and the seriousness on her face melted away his grin. 'I'm on the trail of a German spy,' said Nancy.

Jamie quirked an eyebrow.

'I am!' insisted Nancy. 'His name is Mr. Simpson, and he's a teacher.'

'A teacher?' asked Jamie. 'Why would a teacher be a spy?'

'You don't know him,' said Nancy. 'He's a rotten cruel brute.'

'Sounds like most teachers I know.'

'He wasn't always like that,' said Nancy. 'My sister said he used to be one of the good ones. Not exactly friendly, but not over-fond of the tawse like some of them. But since the war started, he's just got nastier and nastier.'

'That still doesn't make him a spy,' said Jamie. 'Simpson doesn't sound like a German name, for a start.'

'No, well,' said Nancy. 'That's as may be. But I'm sure of it.' She looked at Jamie and realised that she already trusted him. She was a good judge of character, or at least she'd always thought so. 'If I tell you, you can't tell anyone else.'

Jamie nodded.

'Promise?'

'Cross my heart and hope to die,' said Jamie.

'Stick a needle in my eye,' continued Nancy. 'All right. I was wandering around the big houses on the Perth Road one day when I heard someone arguing through an open window. I crept a bit closer to hear what was going on—my ma always said I was nosey—and it was Mr. Simpson, arguing with someone in German. That made me suspicious, so I started following him. And every night he leaves his house and wanders down towards the railway station or the docks.'

'I suppose that's *quite* suspicious,' said Jamie. 'Why didn't you just tell someone instead of trying to follow him yourself?'

Nancy sighed. 'My mother and father said it was all my imagination. So I didn't have any choice, you see. Besides. Everyone else is doing something to help with the war effort, so why shouldn't I?'

Jamie nodded. 'But it's dangerous to be out walking the streets at night.'

Nancy thought for a moment, then said, 'It wouldn't be so dangerous if you came with me.'

'Me?' asked Jamie.

Nancy nodded.

'I don't think so,' said Jamie.

'You *have* to,' said Nancy.

'Oh, do I now?'

'Yes. It's your patriotic duty to help with the war,' said Nancy seriously.

'The war has nothing to do with me. It's stupid and far away.'

Nancy glowered at Jamie. 'Well, I'm going to carry on,' she said. 'If you're too much of a coward, you don't have to.'

'Coward? It's nothing to do with being a coward. I just want to be left alone.'

'Fine. I'll leave you alone, then. Go on back to your cemetery.'

'I said I'd walk you home,' said Jamie.

'I don't want you to,' said Nancy sulkily. They walked on, saying nothing, with Nancy deliberately looking everywhere but at Jamie, and keeping a half step ahead of the boy.

'Look, all right, I'll help,' said Jamie at last.

'You will?' exclaimed Nancy.

Jamie nodded.

'Oh thank you! Meet me at the Howff at ten o'clock tomorrow night.'

'All right,' said Jamie resignedly.

Nancy grinned. 'You'll see,' she said. 'This is important war work.'

Jamie shook his head. He didn't know exactly how she'd roped him in to her crazy scheme, but he supposed it was better that someone was with her to stop her getting into more trouble.

CHAPTER TWO
HMS ARGYLL

HMS *Argyll* surged through the heavy seas, her powerful engines pushing her eleven thousand ton bulk through the waves at a speed of over sixteen knots. The deck rolled under the feet of Midshipman Harry Melville, and not for the first time on his maiden voyage he thanked Providence that he wasn't susceptible to seasickness like some of his compatriots. The wardroom had been full of green faces on this voyage so far, and with the seas getting stormier, it was only going to get worse for the inexperienced sailors.

The *Argyll* had completed her refit at Plymouth, and was on her way to rejoin the 3rd Cruiser Squadron of the Grand Fleet at Rosyth. The quickest way would have been to sail up the East coast, but the North Sea was full of German submarines, so she'd been given orders to sail up the West coast instead, through the Irish Sea, around Cape Wrath and through the Pentland Firth, then South towards the Firth of Forth. Captain James Tancred had pushed them hard on the voyage so far, coaxing extra knots out of the *Argyll*'s engines to ensure that they kept on schedule. With heavy seas and bad weather, that didn't make for a smooth cruise.

Harry was fresh out of the Naval College and had been assigned to the *Argyll*'s complement for the clockwise route around the British Isles as part of his further training. He was expected to spend three years at sea as a midshipman before being commissioned as a sub-lieutenant. As an untrained middy, he imagined he'd be posted to a ship of the Reserve Fleet where he'd be unlikely to face much in the way of combat, but in the meantime, he was on the crew of a ship that formed part of the Grand Fleet, Great Britain's defence against the Imperial German Navy. The *Argyll* wasn't the largest ship in the fleet, but she was a genuine warship capable of long-range independent operations, with the firepower to defeat anything up to battleship size, and the speed to outrun anything she couldn't outgun.

'You there! Middy!' shouted the Officer of the Watch.

'Sir!' responded Harry crisply.

'Let's see what Dartmouth is pushing into your heads these days, Tanky,' said Lieutenant Williams. 'Come and plot a course for Rosyth.'

Harry gulped and stared down at the chart. He'd plotted courses a dozen times—a hundred—while at the Naval College, but never while at sea. Never on a real ship. He'd never been called 'Tanky' before—the nickname given to the Navigator's midshipman assistant, for reasons that seemed obscure to Harry but had probably something to do with navigators traditionally also being responsible for the ship's fresh water tanks.

'Aye aye, sir,' said Harry, which was the only acceptable response to an order from an officer, and set to the task of determining their location and bearing. They'd already threaded the Pentland Firth between Orkney and Caithness, and were heading South towards Fife. In theory it was a simple route, nothing as complicated as the first leg of their journey through the Irish Sea and past the Hebrides with their dozens of tiny islands and reefs and other hazards to navigation. The West coast of Scotland was a jagged mess compared to the smooth lines of the East coast.

Harry sweated over the charts for what seemed like an age, checking and re-checking his figures, then presented his course to the lieutenant.

'Hmm. Not bad,' said the lieutenant. 'You seem familiar with these seas,' he said.

'Yes, sir,' said Harry. 'I'm from Broughty Ferry, and my grandpa was a captain on a Dundee whaler. I know the seas around the Tay and Fife quite well.'

'There's only one problem,' said the lieutenant. He tapped at the chart. 'What do we have here?'

'That's the Inchcape, sir,' said Harry. 'The Bell Rock.'

'And you take us rather close, do you not?'

Harry looked at the course he'd plotted. The course came within a mile of the dangerous reef. 'It's a mile, sir,' he said.

'That's not much of a margin in heavy seas, middy,' said the lieutenant. 'What if the *Argyll*'s course drifts?'

'We'll be able to use the lighthouse for navigation,' said Harry.

'In daylight, maybe,' said the lieutenant. 'But what about at night? We won't make it to the Bell Rock until gone four in the morning.'

Harry frowned. Was that a trick question? 'Um,' he began. 'We'll see the light, won't we, sir?'

The lieutenant shook his head sadly. 'Oh dear. It seems Dartmouth isn't teaching you young gentlemen the realities of warfare. Lighthouses, while a wonderful thing in peacetime, have one enormous drawback in time of war. Can you guess what it is, Mr. Melville?'

Harry thought furiously. Each lighthouse had a specific pattern of flashing light so you could always tell which lighthouse you were looking at. Of course, these patterns weren't secret, so there was nothing to prevent German ships from using the lights for navigation, too.

'Enemy ships can use the lights, sir,' said Harry confidently.

'Not just ships, Mr. Melville,' said the lieutenant. 'Zeppelins. U-boats. The enemy would just love for us to light his way to his targets. We have a hard enough time keeping his ships away without making his job easier by lighting his way right up to our front door. Remember Scarborough? No, we don't switch on the lights unless we really have to. For example, if the fleet were sailing from Scapa Flow, we'd arrange for the lights to be switched on at specific times.'

Harry stared out into the stormy murk. The sea crashed across the bow of the *Argyll* in enormous grey waves that rolled the ship with every impact, and he was glad that he was safe and dry on the bridge. 'Won't they switch the light on for us, sir?'

'That would be up to the captain,' said the lieutenant. 'We've made this journey a dozen times before, so the old man doesn't usually bother. Here, this is the route we're going to take.' He pulled out a chart and laid it on the table on top of Harry's attempt at navigation. 'We'll stay eight miles off the Bell Rock, and get well past the reef before turning in and heading up the Forth for Rosyth.'

Harry peered at the chart. They'd be coming close to his home—the home he hadn't seen for over a year. It was a long, long way from Dartmouth in Devon to Broughty Ferry, and he'd never been able to accumulate enough shore leave to make the trip. It would be strange to be passing so close to Broughty Ferry, so close to his mother and father and little brother. They'd have no inkling that he was just a few miles away. Still, once he was stationed at Rosyth, he'd be a short train ride from Dundee, and could pop home for a visit even if he just had a day pass.

Until he was assigned a new ship, that was.

He'd always known that a sailor spent a lot of time away from home. And that was even more true when there was a war to be fought.

He pushed thoughts of home to one side and went about his duties.

CHAPTER THREE
DUNDEE

Nancy glanced at the clock. It was already quarter to ten. The hours had dragged as she'd waited impatiently for the day to pass, but now she realised that she'd have to hurry if she was to make it all the way into town to meet Jamie before the hour struck. Her pa was out at the bakery, but her ma was upstairs, fast asleep after a long day's work at the hospital. She pulled the front door open, holding her breath and hoping that the hinges didn't squeak.

'And just where do you think *you're* going, Nancy Caird?' Her sister's voice made her jump.

Nancy turned to see Nelly standing in the doorway of the living room, her hands on her hips in a perfect imitation of their mother.

'Be quiet,' said Nancy. 'You'll wake ma.'

'I'll be loud if I want to,' said Nelly. 'I'm not the one sneaking out in the middle of the night.'

Nancy looked her sister up and down. 'No, but you're not long in, are you, Nelly?'

'And what does that have to do with anything?' snapped Nelly.

'Your shift finished at four o'clock. What have you been up to since then?' Nancy could see that Nelly was leaning against the door frame as if she didn't quite trust her balance. 'Is that smudged rouge on your lips?'

'You shut your mouth, Nancy Caird,' said Nelly.

'You can do what you like, as far as I'm concerned,' said Nancy. 'You're fourteen. You've got a job. If you want to be out to all hours, drinking and kissing laddies, that's your decision.' Nancy paused. 'But I'm not sure ma and pa will see it that way.'

Nelly narrowed her eyes at her sister.

'You're a nasty wee thing, you know that?'

Nancy shrugged. She normally got on well with her sister, but tonight was important. She couldn't let Nelly stop her going out, and if the price she had to pay was that her sister was a bit annoyed at her, so be it. In fact, most of the time, Nancy was jealous of Nelly. Not for the drinking and the boys—neither appealed to her at all—but for her job in the jute factory. All right, it was just ropes for army tents she made, but that was a genuine and important part of the war effort. Tents couldn't stay up without ropes. Soldiers couldn't sleep without tents. And soldiers without sleep weren't much use in battle. What was that saying? For want of a nail?

That said, tent ropes weren't as important as tracking

down a spy. 'Good night, Nelly,' said Nancy, and slipped out the door without another word.

It was starting to rain hard, and a cold dampness was soaking through the heavy wool of Nancy's coat. Where *was* Jamie? She'd looked all around the Howff but there was no sign of him. The clock on the church had nearly reached half-past ten.

He'd decided not to come.

Well, no matter. She'd manage on her own. Who needed a dirty smelly tramp like Jamie Balfour? Nancy looked around one more time, then set off towards the Perth Road.

'Wait a minute!' called Jamie, running up behind her.

'And where have you been, Jamie Balfour?' she snapped.

Jamie shrugged. 'I've been busy,' he said.

'Busy? What do you have to do that's more important than catching a spy?' Nancy put her hands on her hips.

'Finding food,' he said.

'Oh! That reminds me.' She glared at Jamie. 'It's your fault. You made me forget that I brought you a pie.' She reached into the pocket of her coat and pulled out a greasy paper package. 'But if you've been finding food, I don't suppose you'll want it now.'

'I *will*,' said Jamie, grabbing at the pie. He pulled

the wrapper off and bit into the crust, the crisp pastry crumbling into his mouth. 'Oh aye,' he said, his mouth full of meat and gristle and grease. 'That's the stuff.'

'You eat like a pig,' said Nancy, secretly admiring the way he stuffed the pie into his face with such obvious enjoyment.

Jamie grinned and took another bite. 'Want a bit?' he asked, his mouth full, holding his hand out to Nancy in a way that made it very obvious that he really wanted her to say 'No'.

Nancy shook her head. 'I've had my tea,' she said. She wondered how long it had been since Jamie had eaten properly. He was all angles and bones. 'Eat up,' she said. 'We have to get going.'

They trudged along the Nethergate in the rain, great streams of water racing along the gutters. Nancy pulled her coat tight around her against the rising wind.

'How do you know it was German?' asked Jamie suddenly.

'How do I know *what* was German?'

'Mr. Simpson. When you heard him having his argument. How do you know he was speaking German?'

'Oh. That's easy. My Uncle Stuart taught me a few words. I recognised "ich bin" and "du bist".' She smiled. 'He always says "du bist mein Schatz" to me.'

'What does that mean?'

'You are my treasure,' said Nancy.

'He sounds like a proper charmer,' said Jamie. 'How does he know German?'

'He's travelled all over the world. France. Italy. America. Africa. Germany. That was before the war, of course. He's back in Dundee now. My pa says he's the black sheep of the family, and he's always getting into trouble, but he's got such wonderful stories.' Nancy sighed. 'He's my favourite uncle.'

'No-one in my family ever went abroad, except for my pa,' said Jamie.

'What, never?' asked Nancy.

Jamie shook his head. 'My grandpa was born, lived, and died in Dundee, and never left the city. He never even went to Fife.'

Nancy nodded. 'My grandpa was the same. My other grandpa—my ma's pa—was from Glasgow, though.'

'I'd like to go to Glasgow one day,' said Jamie. 'But I doubt I ever will.'

'So, what about your pa?' asked Nancy.

Jamie got a far-away look in his eye. 'Aye, he left Dundee. He left Scotland, too.'

'Where did he go?'

Jamie shrugged. 'I don't know,' he said. 'Not exactly. He went away with the Black Watch on a train, and never came back.'

'What happened to him?'

'What difference does it make? He died in one battle or another, hundreds of miles away from my ma and me. They sent us a form with the details, but I couldn't pronounce the name of the place, and my ma threw it into the fire before I could work it out.' He blinked. 'A form. With wee spaces for them to fill in his name and rank and a rubber stamp for the name of the regiment. It wasn't even a real letter.'

'I'm sorry,' said Nancy quietly.

'Aye. Well.'

Nancy decided to change the subject. 'But Glasgow, eh? I'd like to go to Glasgow, too, someday.'

Jamie nodded. It was obvious to Nancy that he regretted talking about his father. 'Someday, maybe,' he said.

'Here we are,' said Nancy. 'I think we're here in time. If Mr. Simpson keeps to his schedule, he should be leaving his house within the next half hour.'

'Let's get under cover,' said Jamie. 'If we've got a wee while to wait, we don't want to get even wetter.'

Nancy didn't think that Jamie could get any wetter. Nancy was dry enough inside her coat, but Jamie's clothes were soaked through and his teeth were starting to chatter with the cold. But she nodded and pointed to a garden gate in a deep archway. 'Under here,' she said. 'It'll be a bit sheltered, and we'll still be able to see him when he comes past.'

Jamie shivered. The longer he stood still, the colder he got.

'Stop fidgeting,' said Nancy.

Jamie made a face. 'I don't fancy waiting out here all night.'

'Somehow, I don't think we'll have to,' said Nancy.

'No?'

Nancy nodded at a tall figure making his way down the road. 'Here he is now...'

CHAPTER FOUR
HMS ARGYLL

Midshipman Harry Melville staggered as the *Argyll* rolled from side to side. He bumped into a chief petty officer whose balance seemed completely unaffected by the heavy seas.

'Sorry, Chief,' said Harry.

The chief petty officer grunted. It wasn't the first time he'd been jostled by a midshipman who hadn't quite found his sea legs, and it wouldn't be the last. 'Be on your way, snotty,' said Chief Roberts. Snotty was the nickname everyone used on midshipmen. It wasn't personal.

'Yes, Chief. Sorry, Chief,' said Harry, and climbed the ladder to the bridge. He was scheduled to be the Midshipman of the Watch on the middle watch, starting at midnight and ending at four in the morning. His duties mostly consisted of keeping notes for the Officer of the Watch, as no-one would entrust a lowly middy with any *real* responsibility, but it was still important work that would be checked in minute detail and any sloppiness punished extensively.

Harry was exhausted. He hadn't had any real sleep for nearly two days, and the strain of sailing the stormy seas was beginning to take its toll on his nerves. He wasn't alone. There was tension on the face of nearly every sailor on board, and it was only hot strong black coffee that kept some of them upright.

Harry relieved his friend Midshipman James 'Dusty' Miller, who looked almost pathetically grateful that his watch had come to an end. Harry stared out into the darkness. The sea spray crashed over the bow of the ship, but beyond that the sea was swallowed up by waves of fog and rain coming in billowing opaque sheets.

'Course?' snapped Captain Tancred. The captain had been on the bridge for over twelve hours, but you wouldn't have been able to tell from his appearance. Harry was sure that if *he'd* been on the bridge that long, he'd have succumbed to the urge to loosen his tie or maybe take his jacket off, but Captain Tancred looked like he was ready for inspection. There didn't even seem to be a shadow of a beard on his face, and Harry wondered how the captain had worked *that* particular piece of magic. In his short time in the Royal Navy, Harry had learned one very important thing—captains were a breed apart, unlike other mortals, and the laws of physics didn't seem to apply to them.

Harry rubbed his own smooth chin. He'd bought

a razor in Plymouth, but so far it didn't seem like he needed it. Maybe soon, though. He was fifteen, after all. A grown man, as near as made no difference.

The navigator rattled off their location, bearing, and speed, and Harry dutifully noted it down in the log.

'We'll pass the Bell Rock by eight miles to the east?' asked the captain.

'Yes, sir,' confirmed the navigator.

The captain rubbed his stubble-less chin. 'I think a belt-and-braces approach is called for,' he said. 'We wouldn't want all this hard work to go to waste. Especially now we're so close to Rosyth.' He nodded at Harry. 'Mr. Melville. Ask the radio room to call the offices of C-in-C Rosyth and request respectfully that we might like a little light from the Bell Rock to see us home.'

'Aye aye, Captain,' said Harry, and rushed off to pass on the message. The order worried him a bit. Wasn't it only a few hours before that Lieutenant Williams had told him that the captain didn't like making a fuss? If he thought conditions were so bad that he had to risk alerting enemy vessels, they must be pretty bad indeed.

Harry made his way to the radio room, a padded and insulated cabin in the depths of the hold, part of the ship that seemed disconnected, its own little island with an umbilical cord to the outside world. The chirp and chatter of the signals flooding the airways leaked from the headphones, and Harry wondered how anyone could ever make sense of it.

Harry delivered the captain's message.

'Will do, lad,' said the telegraph operator. 'Might take a wee while to get a response, though. Do you want to wait?'

'I have to get back to the bridge,' said Harry.

'Right-o,' said the operator, crouching over his telegraph key and tapping it with the finesse of a concert pianist. Harry wobbled his way back up to the captain. He reported that he'd passed the message on, and that the radio room would send a runner with the response as soon as possible.

The captain nodded, and glanced at the ship's clock. It was nearly half-past midnight.

'Keep an eye on my ship, Mr. Melville,' said the captain. 'I'm going to get forty winks, so I'll leave her in your capable hands. But if you get so much as a scratch on her paintwork, I'll be taking it out of your wages.' The captain smiled tiredly at the young midshipman and left the bridge. The Officer of the Watch was in charge of the ship while the captain was off the bridge, of course, but Harry grinned at the thought of being left in command. Someday he would be. Someday he'd have his own ship.

At least, considered Harry, if the captain thought it was safe to leave the bridge, he had to be confident that there weren't going to be any problems between here and Rosyth after all. They'd laid in a course to give the Bell

Rock a wide berth, they'd asked for the lighthouse to be lit, and they'd set a speed that would take them into the Firth of Forth before dawn to avoid the U-boat patrols.

Everything that could be done, had been done.

What's more, Harry didn't think that the Germans would fancy being out at sea in this weather, either. And if the *Argyll* couldn't see beyond the end of her own bow, he doubted any enemy vessels would have much luck spotting them. That was the main reason they'd pushed ahead so quickly—the captain wanted to make it to the Isle of May at the mouth of the Firth of Forth before the German submarines began their dawn patrols.

Just a few more hours, and they'd be safe with the rest of the fleet at Rosyth.

CHAPTER FIVE
DUNDEE

Nancy and Jamie followed Mr. Simpson from Perth Road down the Nethergate, just as Nancy had done the previous night.

'He'll head down Union Street,' said Nancy.

'That's too open,' said Jamie. 'We won't be able to follow. He'll spot us for sure.'

'That's why I lost him last time.'

'Come on,' said Jamie, grabbing Nancy's hand. As Mr. Simpson turned down Union Street, Jamie dragged Nancy further down the Nethergate, past the corner where Mr. Simpson had turned down.

'Here,' said Jamie, pointing to a dark and narrow alleyway. 'Couttie's Wynd. This'll take us down to Whitehall Crescent, then Dock Street. If he's going to the dock, we should be able to catch up with him.'

'What if he's going to the railway station?'

'You said you went there last night, aye?'

Nancy nodded.

'If you didn't see him there last night, chances are he went the other way.'

Nancy nodded again. Jamie was probably right. 'Let's go.'

Couttie's Wynd was dark and the cobblestones were slippery in the rain, but they ran down the alleyway as fast as they could go. They came out onto the street, then turned left and headed for Dock Street.

'Where is he?' said Nancy, looking down the street. 'I don't see him.'

Jamie pulled her into a doorway and put a finger to his lips. He pointed behind them.

'What? Why? Can you—' Nancy closed her mouth suddenly. There he was, his hat pulled down over his face against the rain, his coat collar turned up, but unmistakably him, barely twenty yards away and heading right in their direction. They'd overtaken him when they ran down the alleyway.

Nancy and Jamie held their breath and hugged the shadows until Mr. Simpson had passed. After a few seconds, they emerged from their hiding place and continued following him.

He turned into the open square of Greenmarket, then, glancing around briefly as if checking whether he was being followed, made his way inside one of the big five-storey buildings.

Nancy stared up at the building. From the top floor

you'd have a good view out over the Earl Grey Dock. An ideal place for a spy who was interested in shipping. Maybe she'd been wrong the previous night. Maybe the railway station wasn't the spy's target.

There was a dim light in a ground-floor window, but the rest of the building was dark. Several panes of glass were broken in the upper windows. It looked like the building was abandoned. Nancy crept up to the lit window and Jamie followed close behind.

'Can you hear anything?' asked Jamie.

'Yes. No. I don't know,' said Nancy. 'I can hear *something*.' The window was high, just above the level of Nancy's head. She thought for a second. 'Jamie, can you help me climb up? I need to see what's going on.'

Jamie nodded and made a stirrup of his hands. Nancy stepped into them, then Jamie lifted her up. Nancy grabbed onto the window sill and poked her head up.

Inside was an office, with a battered wooden desk, chairs, and filing cabinets pushed together haphazardly. The light came from a single oil lamp on the desk, where a man sat with his back to the window, an earphone pressed to his head, a notebook and pencil at his right hand.

Mr. Simpson was facing the other man, shaking his hat dry and wiping his face with a handkerchief.

'What's going on?' whispered Jamie.

'Shh.'

'My arms are getting tired.'

'Hold still,' said Nancy, and pushed her head as close to the window as she dared.

Jamie's hands were hurting and his arms began to twitch. Nancy was heavier than she looked, and Jamie's diet over the past few months hadn't been enough to maintain his muscle. He gritted his teeth and braced his legs as best he could.

'Let me down,' said Nancy at last, and Jamie let her drop to the pavement. He shook his arms and tried to rub some feeling back into his hands. 'Well?' he said.

'I couldn't make out much. There were two of them. Mr. Simpson and someone else—I couldn't see his face. They had a radio and were talking about Argyll, and Arbroath, and something about a signal, and I think they said something about a submarine... I couldn't hear every word. I got the impression that something was happening tonight, though.'

'Arbroath's just up the coast, but Argyll's on the other side of the country, isn't it?'

'I think so,' said Nancy, who had never been very good at geography. 'I don't know what it all means.'

'We have to tell someone,' said Jamie.

'A policeman,' said Nancy. 'We have to fetch a policeman.'

Jamie looked doubtful.

'We'll go to the railway station,' said Nancy. 'There's

bound to be a policeman there.'

'I suppose so,' said Jamie, who wasn't popular with Dundee's police. 'Let's go.'

The railway station was quiet, but standing outside the main entrance, just as Nancy had suspected, was a policeman.

'I can't be rushing off on the say-so of you little troublemakers,' said the constable. 'There's an ambulance train coming through here at half-past midnight, and I've got to keep an eye on the place.' He stared at them, his gaze a bit harder and longer when it lingered on Jamie.

'Please, mister,' said Nancy in her best little girl pleading voice. 'Please. It's ever so important. I'm *sure* they're up to no good. Can't you spare just five minutes? It's just up the street.'

Jamie took a half-step back into the shadows and tried to look inconspicuous. The constable's frosty attitude was starting to thaw, but every time he glanced at Jamie the temperature seemed to drop a degree or two. If Nancy could just hold his attention for a little bit longer...

It took another five minutes of pleading, but eventually Nancy wore him down and the constable agreed to come and take a look. Nancy grabbed him by the hand and led him along the street, with Jamie coming up the rear.

'This is it,' said Nancy. The whole building was dark.

The constable peered into the window. 'There's nothing there,' he said.

'Oh, can't we take a look inside?' asked Nancy. 'Please?'

'Don't be silly,' said the constable. 'It's all locked up.'

Jamie pushed at the door and it swung open.

'Here! Don't you be going breaking and entering!' exclaimed the constable.

'It was already open,' said Jamie.

'We should take a look inside,' said Nancy, pushing past Jamie before the constable could object.

The office was empty. Jamie touched the oil lamp. 'It's warm,' he said. 'That proves someone's been here recently.'

The constable lifted up his helmet and scratched his head.

'And look here,' said Nancy, pulling a dust sheet off the radio. 'This is suspicious, isn't it?'

'I don't know,' said the constable.

'It's obvious, isn't it?' said Jamie. 'They're spies. They're using the radio to listen in on the shipping. They're probably signalling German submarines.'

'I don't know about that,' said the constable.

'For goodness' sake, what are you going to do about it?' snapped Jamie.

'Now look here, you young tinker, who are you to tell

me what to do?' The constable peered at Jamie in the gloom. 'You're Jamie the Howff, aren't you?'

'So what if he is?' asked Nancy.

'You don't want to be hanging around with a known thief and liar and troublemaker like this one,' said the constable. 'You be getting home now, young lady. And as for you,' he prodded Jamie in the chest, 'you get out of here now, before I arrest you for wasting police time.'

'But...' began Jamie.

The constable drew back a hand and Jamie flinched. 'Go on. Be off with you. If I didn't have to get back to the station for the ambulance train, you'd be in a lot more trouble.' He grabbed Jamie by the ear and pulled him out into the street.

'Leave him alone,' cried Nancy.

The constable let go of Jamie's ear. 'He's been dragging you into trouble, young lady. Stay away from him, if you know what's good for you.' The constable flipped open his pocket watch and shook his head. 'I've got to be on my way. If I see either of you again tonight, you'll be in big trouble, do you hear?' And with that he was off down the street, his dark-uniformed bulk disappearing into the rainy darkness within seconds.

'I'm sorry,' said Jamie at last.

'It's not your fault,' said Nancy. 'And besides, *I'm* the one who's been dragging *you* into trouble. Show how much *he* knows.'

Jamie managed a half smile. 'So what do we do now? Do we try to find another policeman?'

Nancy shook her head. 'I don't think so,' she said. 'We need someone who's more likely to believe us.'

They stood in the doorway, watching the rain pour down and thinking furiously.

'What about your uncle?' said Jamie.

'My uncle?' said Nancy. 'Yes! Uncle Stuart! He'll believe me—he's probably run into all sorts of spies and plots in his adventures all over the world.'

'Then let's go,' said Jamie.

Nancy nodded. 'It's not far,' she said, and ran off up the street. Jamie followed close behind.

'It's just up here,' said Nancy. 'He's got a house at the end of this street.'

'Then what are we waiting for?' asked Jamie.

'Um,' said Nancy, stopping in her tracks.

'What is it?' asked Jamie.

Nancy looked down at her feet. She couldn't look Jamie in the eye. 'Maybe you'd better stay outside while I talk to my uncle,' she said.

'What? Why?'

'It's just... well, I mean, he doesn't know you, and... um... you saw how the policeman talked to you. I mean, you look like... you look a bit...'

'Oh,' said Jamie, understanding.

'You could wait outside,' suggested Nancy.

Jamie was silent.

'Jamie?' prompted Nancy. 'I'm sorry, Jamie.'

'It's fine,' said Jamie, in a voice that made it obvious that it *wasn't* fine. 'I'll stay outside. I'll stay here in the gutter where I belong.'

'I didn't *say* that, Jamie.'

'No, you go on. It was only my idea to speak to your uncle. I didn't want to help you with this stupid plan anyway.'

'Don't be like that, Jamie.'

He shrugged. 'Seeing as you don't need me, I'll be off,' he said. 'You can carry on without me. I won't embarrass you if I'm not here.' He turned and started trudging away.

'Don't go! Jamie, I'm sorry. Come with me.' Nancy ran after him and grabbed his sleeve. Jamie snatched his arm away. 'Jamie!'

Jamie ignored her and kept walking.

CHAPTER SIX
HMS ARGYLL

Harry felt a prod in the small of his back and turned around to see one of the telegraph operators standing behind him.

'Message,' prompted the sailor, pushing the slip of paper into Harry's hand before disappearing back down the ladder without waiting for a response. A midshipman was technically an officer, but you'd never catch an enlisted man treating him as such. Harry unfolded the message from the radio room and scanned it quickly.

'Sir,' he said to the Officer of the Watch. 'We've had a response from Rosyth command. The Bell Rock lighthouse doesn't have a radio, but they're going to send a motor torpedo boat from Rosyth to pass on the request, and send a message to the shore station at Arbroath. The light will be lit by the time we get to the Bell Rock.'

Lieutenant Williams nodded. 'That should be fine. We've still got plenty of time before we get close.' He pondered for a second. 'You'd better go and tell the captain, though.'

'Aye aye, sir,' said Harry.

Harry climbed down onto the deck and gasped as a gust of icy wind blasted sharp salt spray into his face. The ship was an island in a vast sea of black storminess, a whirling void of sea and rain and wind combined, and the conditions only seemed to be getting worse. Harry looked up at the *Argyll*'s four huge funnels, just aft of the bridge superstructure. The heavy smoke was whipped off into the night as soon as it entered the air, disappearing into the storm. Fortunately for Harry, it wasn't far from the bridge to the captain's cabin—Captain Tancred liked to be within easy reach of the bridge at all times. But that didn't mean that he liked being interrupted, especially when he was trying to get some sleep after many hours navigating treacherous seas, so it was with some trepidation that Harry wiped the spray from his face, adjusted his uniform, and knocked on the hatch.

'Enter,' came the immediate response from inside.

Harry pushed open the hatch. Far from getting some sleep, Captain Tancred was still in full uniform, including jacket and tie, with only his cap removed as a nod towards comfort. The captain sat at his tiny cabin desk, scratching notes into his log. 'Sorry to bother you, sir, but the lieutenant thought you'd want to see this.' He handed the message to the captain.

'Hmm,' said the captain as he read the note. 'I don't

think much of their chances of getting a motor torpedo boat out of the Forth. Not in these seas.'

'No, sir,' agreed Harry. A motor torpedo boat was a small, fast boat, capable of over thirty knots, that could cover the distance between Rosyth and the Bell Rock in no time at all, but could a mere sixty-footer handle such stormy weather? If the sea could toss the eleven thousand tons of the *Argyll* around like a toy in a bathtub, Harry didn't think he'd like to be on board such a small vessel in weather like this.

'I'm sure they'll get the message through somehow, though,' said the captain, seeing the worry on Harry's face. 'We've laid in a good course, and we're making decent speed for the conditions. We'll be in Rosyth in time for breakfast.'

'Yes, sir,' said Harry.

'Back to the bridge with you, middy,' said the captain. 'Keep an eye on my ship.'

'Aye aye, Captain,' said Harry.

When Harry had gone, the captain sat back and sighed. This voyage should have been a piece of cake, but the sea gods kept throwing obstacles in his path. He reached down and twirled the dial on his personal safe. With a clunk he opened the door. He rummaged amongst his personal papers then pulled out a heavy folder.

He'd been entrusted with the updated intelligence

dossier for Admiral Jellicoe, the commander of the Grand Fleet, who was in Rosyth for a secret planning meeting with Admiral Beatty. This dossier contained all the latest information on the disposition of enemy submarines and the movements of the Imperial German Navy's *Hochseeflotte*, the High Seas Fleet. It was essential for the Admiral's plans for fleet operations in the North Sea, and had been considered too sensitive to send by road or by telegraph. Sending it by warship had seemed safer, but that had been before the storm had built up.

Captain Tancred tossed the dossier back into the safe and spun the dial.

Under no circumstances could this dossier make its way into enemy hands.

CHAPTER SEVEN
DUNDEE

Nancy stared at Jamie as he walked away without a backward glance.

'Fine,' she said to the cold night air. 'I don't need you anyway, Jamie Balfour. See if I don't.' She sniffed and blinked back something that definitely wasn't a tear and turned on her heel.

Nancy's Uncle Stuart lived in a big shabby end terrace house just out of the city centre. It lay empty and neglected for weeks or even months at a time when Uncle Stuart went off on his adventures, but since the war had begun the year before, her uncle had been unable to travel as he used to, and had been forced to make a more permanent home in his big house.

She grabbed the door knocker and rapped.

'Nancy? What the devil are you doing out at this time of night?' Uncle Stuart blinked in surprise.

'Can I come in?'

'What?' Uncle Stuart recovered his wits and waved

Nancy in. 'Of course, of course. Come in. Come and sit by the fire.' He took her coat from her and hung it up next to his own dripping raincoat in the hallway, then ushered her into his study, a chaotic maelstrom of books and newspapers and a huge oak desk that groaned under a pile of notebooks and sheaves of paper. A fire was dying in the fireplace, but Uncle Stuart used tongs to pick up a couple of large lumps of coal from the scuttle and drop them on the embers. 'Sit down, sit down,' he urged, sweeping a pile of newspapers from the room's single armchair onto the floor. He poked at the fire and the flames licked at the new lumps of coal.

Nancy sank into the chair gratefully and felt the chill in her bones start to recede. The chair was so soft and comfortable, she felt that she never wanted to leave it. She closed her eyes.

'Does your mother know where you are?' asked Uncle Stuart, perching on the edge of his desk.

'No,' said Nancy without opening her eyes.

'Come on, Nancy. Tell me what's going on. You know you can tell me anything. Are you in some sort of trouble?'

'It's not like that,' said Nancy, opening her eyes and looking right at her uncle. 'But I do need your help.'

She recounted what she'd been up to, hearing Mr. Simpson speaking German, tailing him over several nights, and eventually catching him sneaking about an abandoned building and using a radio. She didn't tell her uncle about Jamie, though. That would just complicate the situation. Jamie always seemed to complicate the situation.

Uncle Stuart's expression was unreadable.

'And the policeman didn't believe you?' asked Uncle Stuart.

Nancy shook her head. 'That's why...' she almost said 'Jamie thought' but stopped herself in time. 'That's why I thought I'd come to see you. You believe me, don't you? You know what to do?'

Uncle Stuart was quiet for a moment.

'Who else have you told?' he asked.

'No-one. Just the policeman, and he didn't believe anything suspicious was going on.'

'Right,' said Uncle Stuart. He got up from the desk and paced around for a few seconds. 'Let me think.'

'It's important, isn't it?' asked Nancy. 'We all have to do our bit. We all have to help in the war. It's our duty.'

'I said *let me think*,' snapped Uncle Stuart, then, seeing Nancy's face fall, he apologised. 'I'm sorry, Nancy. This is just a tricky situation. I think I know what to do, but you're going to have to trust me. Can you do that?'

Nancy nodded. 'Of course,' she said.

'I'm going to have to go and see someone,' said Uncle Stuart. 'Will you be all right waiting here on your own?'

Nancy nodded. 'I'll be fine,' she said. 'But what about ma and pa?'

'I'll get word to them,' said Uncle Stuart. He opened the safe in the corner of his study and rummaged for a second before pulling out a sheaf of papers—banknotes, perhaps?—and a revolver. He flicked through the notes before stuffing them back into the safe, then flipped out the cylinder of the revolver and loaded it with six rounds. He spun the cylinder with a practised air and snapped it shut with a flick of his wrist.

Nancy stared at the weapon. She'd had no idea her uncle owned a gun.

'What's that for?' she said.

'You never know,' said Uncle Stuart, putting the revolver into his jacket pocket, where it bulged dangerously. 'Sometimes it pays to take precautions.' He locked the safe then looked around the study as if wondering whether he needed to take anything else with him.

'You'll be safe here,' he said. 'See if you can get some sleep.'

Nancy nodded. She could already feel her eyes getting heavy from the warmth of the fire and the comfort of the chair.

'I'll be back as soon as I can,' said Uncle Stuart.

Nancy watched her uncle leave the study and pull the door closed behind him. Then, unexpectedly, she heard the unmistakable sound of a key turning in the lock.

Uncle Stuart had locked her in.

Jamie huddled in the shadows, rain streaming down his face. Nancy had disappeared inside the building half an hour before, and there was no sign of any movement.

He couldn't believe that Nancy had treated him the same way that everyone else did. He'd thought that maybe, just maybe, he'd found someone who wouldn't treat him like an outcast. He'd thought that he might even have found a friend for the first time. Hadn't he come up with the idea of telling her uncle about the spies? Hadn't he helped her find the radio? Helped her follow Mr. Simpson? Hadn't he saved her from the lads who wanted to steal her shoes?

And how had she repaid him? By telling him stay outside, like a dog tied up outside a pub.

He hadn't even wanted to help with her stupid spy hunt. What did it matter if Mr. Simpson was spying for the Germans? The whole war was stupid, and the sooner they all killed each other, the better. His pa had gone off to fight for King and country, and what good had it done? Had it ended the war? Had it saved them all from the Kaiser? No. All it had done was get Jamie's pa killed in some muddy foreign field for no reason at all. All it had done was leave Jamie without a pa, and his ma without her man, both of them left lost and alone.

What was the difference between a King and a Kaiser, anyway? The Kaiser had a stupid moustache while the King had a stupid beard. That was it, as far as Jamie could tell. Both men had been responsible for the death of his father.

Jamie ducked further back into the shadows as a horrendous rattling and whirring noise preceded a motor car along the street. It came to a juddering halt right in front of Nancy's uncle's house. The car was long and low, painted black with a silver star on the radiator. It looked fast and sleek. The driver was crouched over the wheel, his hands gripping it fiercely.

The door to the house opened, and the man Jamie assumed was Nancy's Uncle Stuart ran to the car. He yanked the passenger door open.

Jamie crept closer to listen in.

'Where have you been?' said Uncle Stuart. 'I called you twenty minutes ago.'

'It's not easy driving around in this weather,' grumbled the other man. 'Are you sure we have to go all the way to Arbroath?'

'It's our only chance to send the signal,' said Uncle Stuart. 'The office by the docks is compromised.'

'We could take the radio up the coast,' said the man.

Uncle Stuart shook his head. 'I told you. We can't risk going back to the radio. There's already been one policeman sniffing around it tonight. Consider the radio set lost. We'll have to use the contingency plan—go to the shore station in Arbroath and signal from there.'

'But do we have to go tonight? It's a proper storm out there.'

'Of course it has to be tonight!' snapped Uncle Stuart. 'We've had confirmation that the target has passed Cromarty. It'll be at the mouth of the Tay in a matter of hours. We've only got one chance at this. So just shut up and drive.'

The driver put the car into gear with a crunch and pulled away. As the car drove past the one lighted window in the building, the driver's face was illuminated for a fraction of a second, and Jamie's mouth dropped open.

It was Mr. Simpson.

Nancy pulled at the door, but it was solid and immovable. She sighed and looked around the study. Why had her uncle locked her in? Didn't he trust her? What if she needed to pee? She picked up a newspaper from the desk and flicked through it. It seemed to consist mostly of advertisements for war bonds and stories of patriotism, both at home and at the front.

There was one small article that had been underlined in pencil.

CRUISER REFIT COMPLETE

H.M.S. ARGYLL TO RESUME SERVICE

The Secretary of the Admiralty makes the following announcement:—

H.M.S. Argyll, Capt. James C. Tancred, R.N., commanding, completed its refit at Plymouth and will resume operations with immediate effect.

The Argyll, an armoured cruiser of the Devonshire type, was launched at Greenock in 1904 and completed in 1906; her displacement is 10,850 tons, and on her trials her speed was 22.38 knots. She cost £906,000, carries a crew of 655, and is armed with four 7.5 inch, six 6-inch, 20 three-pounder, and two machine guns. She is fitted with two torpedo-tubes.

The Argyll formed part of the detached squadron of cruisers under the command of Rear-Admiral Sir Colin Keppel that escorted the King and Queen on their voyage to India in 1912.

Nine hundred thousand pounds! What an incredible amount of money. Nancy couldn't imagine such a large sum. She wondered how big such a ship must be.

Something was nagging at the back of her mind.

Something was familiar about the article, but she couldn't quite put her finger on it.

Then it came to her. Argyll. She'd heard Mr. Simpson talking about Arbroath and Argyll, but she'd thought they were talking about the *place* on the other side of Scotland. What if they'd been talking about the ship?

But why did her uncle have an underlined article about that same ship?

Nancy was disturbed in her musings by a sharp rap at the window. She pulled the heavy curtains aside and saw Jamie's familiar face. For some reason she wasn't in the least bit surprised.

'We've got to go,' shouted Jamie through the window.

'I can't,' said Nancy. 'I'm locked in.' She shrugged. 'I don't know what to do.'

'Can't you open the window?'

Nancy pulled at the catch, then strained to lift the heavy sash. She shook her head. 'It's stuck. It's been painted closed, I think.'

'Stand back,' said Jamie.

'Why?' asked Nancy, but Jamie had disappeared from sight. She stared into the blackness outside the window, then leapt backwards as a half brick cracked against the window.

'What are you doing?' demanded Nancy.

'Getting you out,' said Jamie. He inspected the window. 'A good crack. One more shot and it'll break.'

Nancy ducked out of the way, and Jamie smashed the pane with the brick, then knocked out the broken shards of glass. Nancy stared open-mouthed at the vandalism.

'That's my uncle's window!' she said.

'Your uncle is working with Mr. Simpson,' said Jamie in a matter-of-fact tone.

'He's... what? He can't be...' Nancy stopped. It made sense, now. That was why he had a newspaper report about a ship that was mentioned on Mr. Simpson's radio. That was why he'd locked her in. That was why he had a revolver.

'Are you coming, or not?' asked Jamie.

Nancy grabbed a blanket from the back of the armchair, folded it, and placed it over the broken edge of the window. Despite Jamie's efforts, there were still some sharp bits sticking out of the frame, and the hole was very small indeed. For once she was glad she was small and skinny. She climbed carefully out, and Jamie helped her to the ground.

Nancy stood shivering in the rain and wind. Her coat was hanging in Uncle Stuart's hallway, out of reach. 'What do we do now?' she asked.

'We have to get to Arbroath,' said Jamie.

'Arbroath? That was the other place mentioned on the radio, wasn't it?'

'And it's where Mr. Simpson and your uncle are going. They said something about a shore station where they could send a signal.'

'Maybe that's the shore station for the lighthouse,' said Nancy. 'My pa took me to see it once.' She paused for a second. 'Jamie, the *Argyll* is a ship, not a place. A warship. I think they're going to try to signal a German ship or submarine with the *Argyll's* position.'

'But why? What's so important about one ship?'

'I don't know. But we have to stop them.'

'That's why we have to get to Arbroath. But Mr. Simpson and your uncle have a car. I don't know how we're going to get there.'

They stood in silence for a moment, each thinking furiously. A whistle in the far distance, brought to them on the stormy winds, cut through the night.

'That's it!' exclaimed Nancy.

Jamie looked up at her, then broke into a smile as he realised what she was thinking.

'The ambulance train!' they said simultaneously.

CHAPTER EIGHT
HMS QUEEN MARY

The Royal Navy battlecruiser HMS *Queen Mary* patrolled the stormy North Sea, nearly thirty thousand tons of armour with the firepower to match. At over seven hundred feet long, she was half again the length of the *Argyll* and carried twice the number of crew.

She was one of the largest ships in the Royal Navy, a vessel with an excellent reputation and several major battles behind her. Her captain, Cecil Prowse, was a stickler for rules and regulations, and his ship was one of the most efficiently-run in the Grand Fleet.

Commander William James took the slip of paper from the sailor and scanned it quickly. 'Captain,' he said.

'Yes, Mr. James?'

'We've received a message from C-in-C Rosyth. HMS *Argyll* is heading south past the Inchcape, and her captain has requested that the light is switched on. Rosyth sent a motor torpedo boat, but when it reached the mouth of the Forth, the storm was so heavy that it couldn't go any further. They had to turn back. Rosyth requests that we make best speed towards the Bell Rock and attempt to signal them.'

The captain nodded. 'It's Tancred in charge of the *Argyll*, these days, isn't it? Took over when Bernard was given the *Venerable*?'

'I believe so, sir.'

'He's a good man. Sound. Reliable. If he says he needs the light, he needs the light. Make it so,' he said. 'Lay in a course for the Bell Rock.'

'Aye aye, Captain,' said the commander.

The *Queen Mary* was deep in the North Sea, and the weather was against her. The bridge crew clung to their stations as the massive ship was tossed on the mountainous waves. After half an hour, the commander reported to his captain.

'Sir, we're heading right into the teeth of this gale, and we're barely making ten knots,' he said. 'It's going to take us hours to reach the light.'

The captain looked at the chart. 'What course is *Argyll* taking?'

'Due South, sir.'

'Then they'll have the wind behind them. We have no chance of making it to the lighthouse before them.' The captain scratched his chin. 'They'll have to send someone else, I'm afraid.'

'Yes, sir,' said the commander.

'Send a message to Rosyth. The sooner we let them know we can't make it, the sooner they can make alternative arrangements. Keep it simple. "Regret that owing to heavy seas I am unable to contact the Bell Rock light"—that should do.'

'Aye aye, Captain,' responded the commander. He wrote the message down and took it to the radio room, where the operators encrypted the communication using the naval code and transmitted it to Rosyth.

The *Queen Mary* resumed her original course, having done all she could, with full confidence that Rosyth would find some alternative way to get the message to the Bell Rock. Unfortunately, at Rosyth, a new shift had begun in the communications office, and the officer on duty didn't make the connection between the *Queen Mary*'s message and the need to get a message to the Bell Rock for the *Argyll*. The officer assumed that Captain Prowse's terse by-the-book message was a routine communication, stamped it as received, and put it into the appropriate file. Rosyth made no further attempts to contact the Bell Rock, or even the *Argyll* to tell Captain Tancred that they'd been unable to contact the lighthouse.

There was no way to contact the Bell Rock directly. The motor torpedo boat from Rosyth had failed to get out of the Forth. HMS *Queen Mary* had been thwarted by heavy seas. And now the *Argyll* was steaming at full speed towards a lighthouse they fully expected to be lit, but was instead shrouded in darkness, fog, rain, and seas that hid a deadly reef in their storm-swept depths.

CHAPTER NINE
AMBULANCE TRAIN

Jamie had been worried that they wouldn't be able to sneak their way onto the train, but in the cold and rainy conditions everyone was so busy trying to get their job done as quickly as possible that no-one noticed him and Nancy climb into a carriage that had been emptied of its wounded soldiers.

The last ambulance pulled away from the station, taking its soldiers to a hospital or some other place—a nursing home, a school, or perhaps just a large house that had been commandeered for the care and rehabilitation of the wounded. The station master blew his whistle, and with a cloud of steam and a screech of piston-driven iron wheels the train pulled out of Dundee and headed along the banks of the Tay towards Broughty Ferry.

'Are we doing the right thing?' asked Jamie. 'Should we be rushing off on our own like this?'

'We tried telling a policeman. We tried telling my uncle.' The disgust was clear on Nancy's face. She felt betrayed by Uncle Stuart. She shook her head. 'We have to do this ourselves.'

'I suppose you're right,' said Jamie. He didn't feel very confident at going up against two grown men. He wasn't afraid of a fight—put three lads his own size in front of him, and he'd go in with fists swinging. But he was all too aware of the difference in strength between himself and one adult, never mind two.

'It's our duty,' said Nancy.

Jamie frowned. He didn't believe in duty. Duty had killed his father. If he and Nancy went chasing after two of the Kaiser's spies, who was to say that *they* wouldn't end up dead, too? He opened his mouth to say something of the sort, but the look on Nancy's face stopped him. She was utterly determined to put this situation right. And he couldn't leave her to face it on her own.

He nodded. 'So, what do we do once we get to Arbroath?' he asked.

Nancy shrugged. 'We'll come up with something.'

Jamie wasn't comforted by her lack of a plan.

'Don't you think...' he began, then was interrupted by the carriage door opening.

'Bit quieter in here, Hector,' said a short, broad soldier in a khaki kilt, his cap at a rakish angle on his head, revealing a long scar along the side of his head, criss-crossed by black stitches. The top of his left ear was missing.

'It is that, Lachlan,' said his companion, a man as skinny at the other was stout, one eye bandaged and his arm in a sling. 'But I am thinking that the young gentleman and his lady might be wanting the carriage to themselves.'

'Och, away, he's not even started shaving,' said Lachlan. Jamie blushed and stared at the floor of the carriage.

'So what would you two be doing on this train at all?' said Hector. 'You don't look like Black Watch to me.'

'I'm sorry,' piped up Nancy. 'Have we got on the wrong train? It was so busy and confusing at the station. We have to go to Arbroath to see our auntie.'

'Arbroath is it? We're stopping at Arbroath right enough,' said Lachlan. 'Hector and me, we're taking our holidays there this year.'

'Aye,' said Hector. 'We've booked five-star rooms at the Arbroath Infirmary.' He rubbed at the skin around his bandaged eye.

'If the gentleman doesn't mind us joining him?' said Lachlan, sitting down opposite Jamie and Nancy.

'No, no, that's fine,' said Nancy, glancing at Jamie, who kept his gaze firmly on the floor. She could see the tension in his jaw. His hands gripped at the seat cushion. 'I'm Nancy, by the way, and this is Jamie.'

'Don't worry yourself,' said Hector, sitting next to his friend. 'Hector,' he pointed to himself, 'and that one there is Lachlan.'

Lachlan and Hector arranged their kit. Lachlan helped his companion, as Hector had difficulty propping up his rifle and kitbag with one arm in a sling.

'Ah, that's better,' said Lachlan. 'There's an awful moaning and groaning in the other carriage.' He pulled his cap from his head and laid it on his lap.

Nancy gestured at the silver badge on the cap. 'You're in the Black Watch, are you?'

'Aye,' said Hector. 'Or, as the Germans like to call us, the Ladies from Hell.' He gestured at his kilt. 'Do you like my skirt? A nice khaki colour. It doesn't show up the trench mud like tartan does.'

'It's the latest fashion,' said Lachlan.

'I don't know how you can joke about it,' said Jamie quietly.

'Sorry, laddie? What did you say?' asked Hector.

'I said,' repeated Jamie, 'I don't know how you can joke about taking holidays in hospitals and wearing kilts that don't show up the mud. What's wrong with you? There are men dying out there in France!'

'Now, listen here,' said Lachlan.

'No, wait, he's sorry,' interrupted Nancy. 'Don't mind him.' She laid a hand on Jamie's arm and he flinched.

'I'm not...' started Jamie. Nancy gripped his arm hard.

'He's not used to being around soldiers. Not since his pa...' she trailed off.

'Ah. Right,' said Lachlan. 'Listen, laddie, you don't

need to be paying me and Hector any mind. It's just the way we are, you know? When you've seen some of the things we've seen, you either laugh about them, or they cart you off to the funny farm.'

'Your pa,' asked Hector, 'was he in France?'

Jamie nodded.

'And he didn't come back?'

Jamie shook his head.

'I'm sorry, laddie. I am. He's not the only one. My wee brother joined up with me, the daft bugger, but he won't be coming back, either.'

'Nor my cousin Hamish,' said Lachlan. 'There's a village just outside Dornoch that is only getting two soldiers back out of the ten who took the King's shilling.'

'And not all of those two, either,' said Hector, gesturing to his face. 'I left one of my eyes on the fields of Neuve-Chapelle, and Lachlan's short most of an ear.'

'I'm sorry,' said Jamie.

'Ah, don't worry about it,' said Lachlan.

'No,' said Jamie. 'I mean it. I'm sorry. I can't imagine what you've been through.'

Lachlan shrugged. 'The battle was back in March. We're just glad to be out of France and back in Scotland for a wee while.'

'Aye,' said Hector. 'It's good to be back. I don't know why they couldn't send us somewhere civilised like the Highlands, though. I mean, what's in Arbroath?'

'Smokies,' said Lachlan. 'I'll not be happy if we don't get fed Arbroath smokies at least once a day while we're there.'

'Ach,' said Hector. 'I'm not keen. Smoked fish tastes like chimneys.'

'You've no idea what you're talking about,' said Lachlan.

Nancy released her grip on Jamie's arm. He looked at her in gratitude. He'd been about to let his stupid mouth get the better of him, and not for the first time. Nancy had stepped in and stopped him making even more of an idiot of himself.

They sat back in their seats and listened to Lachlan and Hector argue in their soft Highland accents about the relative merits of poached or smoked haddock. Before long, the train was pulling into Arbroath station.

CHAPTER TEN
HMS ARGYLL

Harry didn't want to be on the deck of the *Argyll*. He was soaked to the skin, freezing cold, and his eyes ached from peering into the black void that enveloped the ship. He stood at the high bow of the cruiser, his fingers numb from grasping the icy railing. Every time a wave crashed against the ship, he gasped as the breath was knocked out of him, but every time he resolutely wiped the salt spray out of his eyes and carried on scanning the darkness, looking for the glimmer of the light in the distance.

He kept his attention over to the starboard side, as that's where he expected the light to appear if they'd kept their course straight. With no visible aids they'd been navigating by dead reckoning, but in the rolling seas and constantly shifting conditions it was tricky to keep the ship headed along the bearing marked out by the compass, and at times working out her speed was more a matter of guesswork than science. Harry was beginning to understand the difference between his idealised navigation lessons and the more complicated realities of guiding eleven thousand tons of warship through stormy oceans. You could plan out a route as elegantly as you liked, but getting the ship to follow it when you couldn't see beyond the ship's bow was another matter entirely.

Where *was* that blasted light? He pulled out his binoculars and tried to scan the horizon, but the wind and spray made it impossible to tell if he was even pointing the lenses in the right direction. He let the binoculars fall to his chest and stared out into the night again. The basic eyeball had been good enough for Nelson, and he'd only had one.

Harry thought about Rosyth, where the rest of the fleet was stationed. He'd heard from the other sailors that a ship on station was a very different place from a ship at sea. For a start, there was shore leave. While the other sailors would probably spend their leave arranging rugby matches, or smoking and drinking in the pub, he was much more interested in getting home to Broughty Ferry to see his parents and little brother.

He was looking forward to the routine of lessons, too. A midshipman was a half-formed thing, a boy in a man's uniform, ready to be moulded into an officer. There would be gunnery lessons, covering both firing and maintaining the huge guns. Harry had watched seamen strip one of the six-inch guns on the *Argyll* before they'd set off from Plymouth, and it seemed a daunting—but fascinating—task. There would be signals lessons, including Morse and semaphore. Navigation. Seamanship. Engineering. He'd learn to stand watch in the engine room and the boiler room.

Then there would be all the usual drills that the captain used to keep the ship and its crew at peak readiness. Gunnery drills and navigation drills. Search light control and torpedo drills. All of which would be needed when Admiral Jellicoe called on them to go out and face the German Imperial Navy.

Harry didn't know if he'd still be on the *Argyll* when that happened. It depended on whether he'd be considered a liability. The *Argyll* wasn't a training ship— it was a warship destined for combat. If the captain considered that a bunch of half-trained midshipmen would be a distraction, or would take up too much of his officers' time, he'd simply transfer them, *en masse*, to a ship in the Reserve Fleet as soon as he got to Rosyth. Admiral Jellicoe had been known to leave a ship in port if he didn't think the crew were up to the job, and no captain would want to risk that.

Harry was surprised to realise that he didn't want to leave the *Argyll*. He'd only been on board for a matter of days, but already he felt that she was *his* ship. He'd formed an attachment to the cruiser and her crew that he'd never expected, and the thought of having to leave them left a hollow feeling in his stomach. That was Navy life, of course. You didn't get a say in where you were posted—you just followed orders.

But still, if Harry was given the choice, he'd choose to stay right where he was.

By which he meant on the *Argyll*, not wedged against the railings on her bow in gale-force winds and treacherous seas, staring into black nothingness with his eyes crusted and stinging with salt, the stench of coal smoke burning in his throat. On the *Argyll* was fine, but preferably on the bridge doing navigation drills, or in the wardroom watching Charlie Chaplin movies with his mates, or in the mess playing cards and losing half his wages, or in the gunhouse of the turret watching the shells describe enormous arcs through the air. Anywhere, that is, where it was warm and dry.

There was still no sign of the Bell Rock light. Harry wondered how far away the light would be visible through the thick curtains of rain. Surely they had to be within sight by now?

'Harry!' came a shout in his ear, barely audible above the sound of crashing waves and howling wind. Harry turned, blinking the spray out of his eyes, to see Midshipman Miller standing right next to him, his face scrunched up against the deluge. 'You're relieved. The lieutenant wants you on the bridge.'

'Thank you!' managed Harry, passing the binoculars

carefully to his shipmate. 'Just remember, Dusty. Hold tight, and keep your eyes open.'

'I will that,' muttered Dusty grimly, taking Harry's place and staring out into the whirling storm.

CHAPTER ELEVEN
ARBROATH SIGNAL TOWER

Arbroath railway station wasn't quite as busy as Dundee had been—most of the wounded soldiers had been taken off at Dundee, as Arbroath didn't have the facilities to deal with so many. But it was still busy with the walking wounded like Lachlan and Hector, and a few more serious cases.

'Ach,' said Hector. 'Look at the queue for the ambulances. They've not brought enough cars. We'll be here for hours.'

Lachlan shook his head. 'Nothing else for it,' he said, and pulled out a pack of Woodbines. 'We'll just sit here and have a wee smoke,' he said, planting himself on a bench. 'It's been a long trip from France. If it takes a while longer, it takes a while longer. At least we're back on Scottish soil.'

Hector grunted. 'I'll not feel comfortable until we're back in the Highlands,' he said. 'They're a strange bunch, these lowlanders.' He looked at Nancy and

Jamie. 'No offence intended.'

'None taken,' said Nancy. 'We've got to be on our way. Our auntie will be wondering where we've got to.'

'You take care,' said Lachlan. 'It's a terrible night out there.'

'Thank you, we will,' said Nancy. 'I hope you both get better soon.'

'The doctor said my eye would grow back in no time at all,' said Hector. 'And he was very encouraging about my arm. "Will I be able to play the fiddle, Doctor?" I asked him. "I see no reason why not," he said. Which is grand, because I never could play before.'

Lachlan chortled.

'Good luck,' said Jamie seriously, and stuck out his hand.

Lachlan and Hector shook it in turn.

'Aye,' said Lachlan. 'You too, laddie.'

Outside the railway station, a harassed porter pointed them in the direction of the lighthouse shore station. 'Right that way,' he said. 'It's about half a mile. Keep heading towards the sea and you can't miss it. You'll see the great white tower when you get near the shore.'

They thanked him and set off down the street.

'There's the car,' said Jamie as they drew close.

'Are you sure?' asked Nancy.

Jamie nodded. 'That's the car all right. It has the same silver star on the radiator.' There was no sign of Mr.

Simpson or Uncle Stuart. 'They must be inside already.'

'What do we do now?' asked Nancy.

'I was hoping you'd have an idea,' said Jamie. 'You're the brains of this outfit.'

Nancy cracked a small smile and was glad that Jamie couldn't see her blush in the darkness. She frowned. 'I think we're going to have to go and get someone,' she said.

'That didn't work too well last time,' said Jamie. 'But that was my fault.'

'No,' said Nancy firmly. 'It wasn't your fault at all. It was the stupid fat policeman.'

'Tell you what,' said Jamie. 'You go and get help. I'll wait here and keep an eye on things.'

'Are you sure?' asked Nancy.

Jamie nodded.

'You won't do anything daft?' asked Nancy.

'Like what?'

'Like go into the station before I get back. You wouldn't stand a chance against two grown-ups.'

Jamie shook his head. 'I'll wait out here. I promise.' He shooed Nancy. 'Now go on. Hurry back.'

Nancy frowned at Jamie. She didn't trust him to be sensible.

'Go!' said Jamie.

'I'll be back as quickly as I can,' she said, then rushed off into the night.

Jamie waited for her to go, then looked up at the shore station tower. It was like a miniature lighthouse itself, albeit lacking a light: a round white tower two storeys high, rising out of a single-storey building, with crenellations like a castle and a tall spike on top.

Mr. Simpson and Nancy's Uncle Stuart had no idea who he was. They'd never seen him before. If he went in, maybe he could keep them occupied or slow them down—whatever it was they were doing. Jamie had no idea how long it would take Nancy to find a policeman willing to follow her.

There was no time to waste. He was going in.

The front door was open, and there was darkness beyond in the hallway. Jamie crept in and stopped, cocking his head to listen.

He could hear voices above him, up in the tower. He couldn't quite make out what they were saying, but the discussion sounded quite heated. He climbed the stairs, his soaking wet shoes making damp squelching noises with every step. He ran his hand along the wall as he climbed, counting each step under his breath.

At the top of the stairs was a round room. Jamie peeked over the lip of the stairwell. A middle-aged man in a heavy knit jumper was sitting on a chair, his arms tied behind his back with thick rope.

'I've told you,' said the man. 'I can't contact the lighthouse unless the keepers are watching. I haven't been able to get them to switch the light on.'

'Just tell us where the signal lamp is,' said Uncle Stuart.

'What good will that do you? They're not watching. They'll be huddled up inside in this weather, if they've got any sense.'

Uncle Stuart slapped the man across the face. 'Just tell us.'

'You can't be messing with official equipment!' said the man. 'I'm the Master of the Tender, and it's my solemn duty to ensure that the lighthouse is kept operational at all times.'

'Would you listen to him?' chimed in Mr. Simpson. 'Solemn duty indeed. You're just a nobody.'

'*In salutem omnium*,' said the Master. 'Do you know what that means?'

Mr. Simpson snorted. 'I'm not sure I care.'

'It means *for the safety of all*, and it's the motto of the Northern Lighthouse Board. It's a motto I take very seriously.'

'Just tell us where the signalling lamp is!' shouted Uncle Stuart.

Jamie chuckled under his breath. The officious wee Master was doing a better job of delaying the two spies than he could ever have managed.

'I've told you,' said the Master firmly. 'That's official

76

lighthouse board equipment, and you're not authorised to use it.'

'Oh for goodness' sake,' said Uncle Stuart. 'Simpson. Get up there and have a look.' He pointed to a ladder leading to a hatch in the ceiling. 'Check in the lockers. Force them open if you have to.'

Mr. Simpson nodded and climbed the ladder. A heavy bolt secured the hatch, and he struggled for a moment before managing to pull it. He disappeared up onto the roof of the tower, leaving a blast of rain and wind in his wake.

'If I could have signalled the tower, I would have,' said the Master.

'It's not the tower we want to signal,' said Uncle Stuart.

'Then what?' asked the Master.

'None of your business,' said Uncle Stuart.

Jamie knew—or suspected—who it was they wanted to signal. There had to be a German submarine out there waiting for a message. Mr. Simpson and Uncle Stuart had intercepted a message about a ship, and they expected it to sail past the Tay. If they could get that information to the submarine, it would be able to hunt the ship down even in the dark.

Hundreds of lives were at stake. Jamie had no idea how much longer Nancy was going to take fetching help, so he had to do something to slow them down.

'All right, boss?' he said cheerily as he climbed

nonchalantly into the room, his hands casually in his pockets. 'What's going on?'

CHAPTER TWELVE
HMS ARGYLL

Harry was glad to be back on the bridge, out of the storm, but felt slightly guilty that so many of his shipmates were out on the deck. Lieutenant Williams was Officer of the Watch, and Harry could tell from the way he was nervously tapping his fingernails against the bulkhead that he had expected to see the light of the Bell Rock long before.

'They can't have lit it yet, sir,' said Harry.

'Either that or we've been going a lot more slowly than we think,' responded the lieutenant. 'Of the two, I'd prefer that the light wasn't lit. We *have* to get into the Forth before the German patrols get their beady eyes on us. But no. I fear we're not in range of the light yet.' He sighed. 'If I dared, I'd try to wring a bit more speed out of her.'

'It's filthy black out there, sir,' said Harry. 'It's a powerful light the Bell Rock has, but in these conditions it might not be visible from such a distance.'

'It's also possible that we've drifted off course to the East, and we're even further from the lighthouse than we think,' said the lieutenant. 'Blast this storm!' He shook his head. 'Mr. Melville, go and rouse the rest of the midshipmen from the wardroom. I want every eye available on deck.'

'Aye aye, sir,' said Harry, and ducked back out into the night. The ladder from the bridge was slick with sea and rain, and Harry nearly slipped twice on his way down to the deck. The *Argyll* was still rolling about on the seas, but Harry thought that maybe the storm was lessening just a fraction. He raced along the deck to the stern of the ship as fast as he dared.

'Up and at them, lads!' he shouted as he entered the wardroom. 'All hands on deck.'

The *Argyll* had six midshipmen, three in the Starboard division and three in the Port division—the two divisions rotated the watches under normal circumstances, so that only half the midshipmen were on duty at any one time. Harry, Dusty Miller, and Midshipman Bertram Finch from the Starboard division were already on duty, which left Eric Parker, Herbert Daniels and Roderick Douglas-Hamilton from the Port division in the wardroom.

'Go to blazes, Harry,' mumbled Parker.

'Lieutenant's orders, Nosey,' said Harry. Every sailor with the surname 'Parker' since time immemorial had been known as 'Nosey', with no exceptions. 'We need your sharp eyes at the lookouts so we don't go running right into the docks at Leith.'

Nosey Parker grunted, then turned over and pulled the blanket over his head. Harry kicked his feet.

'Oi!' complained Nosey.

'Get up, then,' said Harry. 'Herbert? Are you awake?'

Daniels lifted his head from his pillow and gave Harry a glare that could have curdled milk before grudgingly slapping his feet onto the deck. Harry nodded his thanks.

'You too, Roderick,' said Harry to the last of the midshipmen. 'I see you there trying to look like a pile of laundry in your bunk.'

Douglas-Hamilton poked his nose outside the covers. 'I say, Melville, old thing, don't be such a beast.'

'Get yourself up and dressed, quick sharp,' said Harry.

The midshipmen grumbled but got themselves together. Harry stayed just long enough to make sure that they weren't going to climb back into their warm bunks, then headed back to the bridge.

Harry knew how his shipmates felt. Sleep was hard enough to come by on a ship in heavy seas without being rudely awoken and dragged out on deck into a freezing storm. He stared into the impenetrable murk that surrounded the ship. If there was a light out there, it might take everyone's eyes on deck to spot it.

Back on the bridge, Harry wiped his face dry with his sleeve and reported back to the lieutenant.

'We've done what we can, Harry,' said the lieutenant.
Harry nodded. 'Yes, sir.'
'It's in the hands of Neptune, now.'

Harry glanced at the clock. It was just after 0400, which would normally mark the end of the Middle watch. He didn't think he'd be going off duty any time soon. Everyone was on the bridge or on deck, hoping to see the glimmer of the Bell Rock lighthouse. The sun wasn't due to rise until after 0700, and the tension on the ship was almost unbearable. Harry didn't think he'd seen so many nervous faces before.

The only thing that gave Harry any consolation was that the weather seemed to be improving. Perhaps if the storm eased up enough, they'd be able to see the light in the distance.

Harry scribbled a routine note in the log, and was painfully aware of how loud his pen sounded scratching against the paper. If it hadn't been for the lieutenant's nervous tapping and the sound of the storm outside, it would have been silent in the bridge save for whispered comments. It was as if the whole ship was holding its breath as it surged forward. Harry felt the inky blackness press down on the ship, like the air itself was as thick and dark as tar. The world didn't exist beyond the bow of the *Argyll*. There was just the ship, alone, on an endless ocean of nothingness.

Without warning, the squall dropped away like a stage curtain. From on deck came a cry, relayed from man to man: 'Sailing ship ahead!'

Seconds later, the captain rushed onto the bridge. 'Report, Lieutenant!' he commanded.

'Sailing ship spotted, sir,' said Lieutenant Williams.

'Where?' asked the captain.

'There,' said the navigator, pointing ahead.

Harry rushed to the window. Almost dead ahead was a ghostly pale shape, towering in the distance. That wasn't a ship's sail!

'That's no ship,' shouted Harry. 'That's the Bell Rock!'

'Helm hard to port,' commanded the captain. 'Engines full astern!'

The *Argyll* shook and bucked as she tried to steer around the lighthouse, her engines vibrating throughout the entire ship as she threw her twin screws into full reverse, but it wasn't enough. Harry watched in horror as the pale spectre of the granite pillar of the Bell Rock lighthouse loomed closer and closer. The *Argyll's* rudder was hard over, desperately trying to turn the ship away from disaster. Degree by degree the ship swung around as they lurched through the screaming waves. For a moment Harry thought that they were going to make it.

Then the *Argyll* crashed into the hidden reef on which the lighthouse was built. With a terrible screeching of tearing metal, the *Argyll* ground to a halt, the razor-sharp rocks shredding her hull, then lurched forward again, throwing the crew to the deck, before coming to a final stop with her keel wedged onto the reef.

CHAPTER THIRTEEN
ARBROATH SIGNAL TOWER

'What do you want?' asked Uncle Stuart. 'Can't you see we're busy? Clear off!'

Jamie took a tentative step into the room and looked around, wondering how he could keep Uncle Stuart and Mr. Simpson occupied. 'What's going on with the chair and the rope? Is it some kind of game? Is it escapology? Like that Harry Houdini? I love Harry Houdini!'

'Get lost,' said Uncle Stuart.

'Ah, go on, show us your trick,' said Jamie. 'I want to see how it's done. Is it trick ropes?'

'Just be on your way before I get angry,' said Uncle Stuart. 'Tell him, Master. Tell him to go before he really, really regrets it.'

'It's hit the reef!' shouted Mr. Simpson from above, climbing down the ladder with a telescope in his hand.

'What?' exclaimed Uncle Stuart.

'I was trying to make out the lighthouse through the storm, and I saw it happen. The ship just ploughed into the rocks. I've never seen anything like it in my life!'

Jamie looked from man to man. He'd hoped to slow down their plans, perhaps by making them maintain some pretence, but it looked like they'd been overtaken by circumstances.

'That's terrible!' said Jamie. 'I'll away and call the coastguard.' He made for the stairs but Uncle Stuart was too quick, and grabbed Jamie by the collar of his shirt.

'Let me go!' he shouted.

'You just wait a wee minute,' said Uncle Stuart. He twisted Jamie's arm up behind his back, and Jamie squeaked in pain.

'Who's the boy?' said Mr. Simpson.

'He's nobody,' said Uncle Stuart.

'Get off! You're hurting me!' said Jamie.

'Stop struggling,' said Uncle Stuart. 'Simpson. Are you sure it's the *Argyll*?'

Mr. Simpson nodded.

Uncle Stuart looked deep in thought. 'You know, this really couldn't be more fortuitous. We'd planned to give the submarine the ship's rough course and schedule, but this is even better! We can give them the exact location. They won't even have to hunt. But we have to move quickly. Someone could notice the wreck at any moment and call the coastguard like our young friend here intended to. We have to signal the submarine *now*.'

'I found the telescope, but I couldn't see the signal lamp.'

'Oh for goodness' sake. It must be up there somewhere,' said Uncle Stuart. 'Keep hold of this one while I look.'

Mr. Simpson took a firm grip of Jamie's upper arm. 'Hurry up, Caird,' he said to Uncle Stuart as Jamie tried to pull away. 'He's a bit of a wriggler.'

Uncle Stuart gave him a fierce glare then climbed the ladder to the roof.

'What's going on?' asked Jamie in his most clueless schoolboy voice. 'I've got to be getting back. My ma will be wondering where I am.'

'Be quiet,' said Mr. Simpson in a distracted voice, then stared Jamie in the eye. 'What are you doing here, anyway?'

'Just running a message for the boss here,' said Jamie. The Master raised his eyebrows slightly at this.

'Is that right?' asked Mr. Simpson, looking at the Master, who quickly disguised his look of surprise.

Jamie nodded almost imperceptibly at the Master, as if to tell him to play along.

'Aye, that's right. The lad just runs messages from the town,' said the Master.

'It's gone four in the morning,' said Mr. Simpson.

Jamie shrugged. 'Doesn't bother me,' he said. 'I like being up all night.'

'Look,' said Mr. Simpson, 'something about this

87

doesn't add up. What are you up to? What's the message you were supposed to deliver?'

Jamie shook his head. 'I'm not telling *you*,' he said. 'Not now you're being so rude.'

Mr. Simpson grabbed Jamie's arm a bit more tightly.

'Get off,' said Jamie. 'You're hurting me.'

'You're up to something, I can tell,' said Mr. Simpson. 'Tell me what you're up to. Tell me *now*.'

Jamie looked up into the man's eyes. He could see the fear there. He could see a man who was out of his depth and starting to panic. The longer Uncle Stuart was out of the room, the more fidgety and tense Mr. Simpson became. A nerve in his jaw was twitching, and his eyes roamed everywhere, as if he expected to be set upon any second.

'Wouldn't *you* like to know,' said Jamie, grinning.

Mr. Simpson took a half step backwards, and for a fraction of a second his grip on Jamie's arm loosened slightly. Jamie took the opportunity to stamp down, hard, on the top of Mr. Simpson's foot. The man yelled with pain and Jamie wrenched his arm free. He took two quick steps to the top of the stairs, but Mr. Simpson had recovered and was on his heels. The man grabbed at Jamie's collar, missed, caught hold of his shoulder and spun him around. Jamie's wet shoes slipped across the floor and he felt his feet slide out from underneath him. With a thud he landed on the floor, cracking his elbow against the hard slabs, the pain shooting up his arm and throughout his body, jangling every nerve. Still he scrambled to the stairs, but Mr. Simpson was on top of him, pressing him to the ground, his face up against Jamie's.

'Got you now,' said Mr. Simpson. Jamie flinched as the stench of Mr. Simpson's breath hit him as hard as a slap, and shut his eyes against the pockmarked sight of the man's oily pale face.

'Leave the lad alone!' shouted the Master.

Jamie managed to get his arms free and flailed his fists, catching Mr. Simpson a crunching blow to the side of the head that rattled his teeth. Jamie scrambled out from underneath him, but Mr. Simpson grabbed hold of his feet and pulled him back into the centre of the room.

'Stay still!' shouted Mr. Simpson. 'Stop struggling!'

Jamie wrenched one foot out of the man's grip, leaving his shoe behind, and kicked up right between Mr. Simpson's legs. The man made an 'oof' sound and sank to his knees. Jamie tried to scramble backwards but Mr. Simpson, gasping from the pain and shock, managed to grab one of his legs again. Jamie kicked and twisted and snarled, but Mr. Simpson held on tightly.

Jamie swung his fists as hard as he could, but the man was taking no nonsense any more and gripped Jamie's leg, his sharp nails digging through the thin material of Jamie's trousers and gouging furrows in his skin. Jamie flailed about as if he were having a fit, but Mr. Simpson's grip remained strong.

'Stop that,' came Uncle Stuart's voice, and Jamie felt something cold and metallic press into the side of his head. Something cold and metallic like the barrel of a pistol.

CHAPTER FOURTEEN
HMS ARGYLL

The bridge of the *Argyll* was pandemonium. Harry didn't know if he was still supposed to be taking notes in the log under the circumstances. Naval College hadn't quite covered this situation.

'I will have ORDER!' bellowed Captain Tancred, and the bridge fell silent. 'Lieutenant Williams, I need damage assessment immediately.'

'Aye aye, Captain,' said the lieutenant. 'Melville, you're with me. Bring your notebook.'

Harry nodded and hurried after the lieutenant.

The situation below decks wasn't good. The *Argyll* had still been going at over 12 knots when she hit the reef, and coming to an abrupt halt had ripped her hull to pieces. Her bottom was pierced in the No. 2 stokehold, where water was now gushing in, and the oil leaking from her damaged tanks had started a fire that was threatening to burn whatever parts of the ship weren't being flooded.

She was so tightly wedged into the reef that she was in no imminent danger of sinking, but the fire was a real risk.

'Melville! Get a fire team together. We've got to extinguish this before the whole ship goes up.'

Harry nodded, all naval discipline and forms of acknowledgement forgotten, and rushed to put together a group of men to tackle the blaze. Lieutenant Williams ran off down the corridor to continue his inspection of the ship, leaving the fire to Harry.

Harry stopped and looked around, coughing and wheezing from the burning oil fumes. He couldn't put out the fire on his own, but where was he going to get a team? The corridor was empty. 'Just pick a direction, Harry,' he said to himself, and ran towards the nearest hatch. He came to a halt, barely stopping himself from running into a solid figure blocking the passage.

'Chief!' exclaimed Harry, relief in his voice, recognising Chief Roberts, the petty officer he'd bumped into earlier. 'We need to get this fire put out!'

The chief looked at Harry with a smile playing about his lips. 'Well, thank goodness for midshipmen. I was planning on roasting some potatoes, and maybe doing a wee bit of toast.'

He stepped to one side, and a stream of sailors came through the hatch, carrying their firefighting gear. Of course. The chief had seen the problem and put a team together before Harry had even had time to panic properly.

'You can stay to supervise if you want,' said the chief, and Harry recognised the gentle mockery in his words.

'That's fine, Chief,' said Harry. 'I can see that you've got things under control. I'd better be heading back to the bridge.'

'You do that, lad,' said the chief. 'Just don't forget about us down here. If you decide to take a little trip, don't leave us behind.'

'Don't worry,' said Harry. 'If we can get this fire out, I think we'll be safe for a little while. We're wedged good and proper onto the reef. Even with the hole in our hull, we're not going to sink.'

'Unless the tide lifts us,' said the chief.

'We're already at high water,' said Harry.

'So what happens when the water drops?' asked the chief. 'When all the weight that was supported by the water weighs down instead on the reef?'

Harry felt a bit nauseous at the thought. 'We'll snap,' said Harry.

'Aye,' said the chief. 'So like I said. When you start planning your little day excursion, don't forget to include us below decks.'

'We won't,' said Harry. 'Thanks, Chief. I'll see you later.'

Harry made his way back to the deck. By now there were sailors rushing everywhere, trying to repair damage and keep the *Argyll* from burning or flooding. It was strange to be walking on the deck without the roll of the sea. It was the first time that Harry had felt a stable surface beneath his feet since they'd left Plymouth, and he came to the sudden realisation that he didn't like the feeling at all. It didn't seem natural. A ship should roll, blast it!

He chuckled to himself, despite the situation. Maybe he was becoming a proper sailor after all.

Harry stared out at the pillar of the Bell Rock lighthouse, barely a hundred yards off the *Argyll*'s bow. Lighthouses were supposed to provide safety, but instead they'd nearly ploughed straight into this one. Where were the keepers? Surely they'd heard the ship as it hit the rocks?

Harry climbed the ladder to the bridge. Lieutenant Williams was making his damage report, and it sounded bad.

'Do you concur, Mr. Melville?' asked the captain.

'Who, me, sir?' said Harry, surprised.

'Yes, you. You've been below decks. What's your opinion of our status?'

'Sir. I spoke to some of the senior crew. It's their opinion the *Argyll* is in danger of breaking up on the reef. Or we could be swept clear of the reef and sink.'

'And what is *your* opinion, Mr. Melville?' asked the captain.

'I trust the crew's opinion, sir. They have far more experience than I do.'

'Good,' said the captain with a thin smile. 'You'll learn that a good crew is the best asset a captain can have. And we have a *very* good crew.' He sighed. 'Take a message to the radio room.'

Harry grabbed a pencil and paper. 'Go ahead, sir.'

'Urgent. *ARGYLL* ashore on Bell Rock. Ship badly damaged. Afraid will rip her bottom as the tide falls. Appears there is no chance of saving the ship.'

Harry felt his throat tighten with fear when the captain spoke those last few words. No chance of saving the ship. It seemed so much more real when it was the captain who said it, and not just the nagging voice in Harry's own head.

'Quick now,' said the captain. 'I fear we don't have any time to lose.'

CHAPTER FIFTEEN
ARBROATH

Nancy ran through the streets of Arbroath, wondering where she was going to get help. Her uncle had a pistol, and maybe Mr. Simpson had one too. Would even a policeman be able to help? If not a policeman, then who? Not that it looked like she had much choice. It was gone half past four in the morning, and the streets were empty.

She just hoped Jamie wasn't doing anything stupid while she wasn't around to keep an eye on him.

Nancy still couldn't believe that it was her own uncle, her lovely, friendly, chatty uncle, Uncle Stuart of the thousand and one tall tales, who was the spy. He'd always had a wild streak, according to Nancy's pa, but there was a difference between going on adventures around the world and being a traitor to your own country. Nancy didn't know how anyone could do that. Did he have no patriotism at all? Didn't he know what was at stake?

She came to the end of the road. Left or right? Maybe

she should go to the train station, even though all the soldiers would have long gone. Perhaps there would still be a policeman.

She wished she didn't feel so helpless.

'Hey!' came a voice from behind her. 'You! Girl! What are you doing out so late?'

Nancy turned to see the scowling expression of a woman, maybe in her thirties, with a strong, plain face, a broad hat shading her eyes, and the collar of her long coat turned up against the rain and wind.

'I'm sorry,' said Nancy. 'I've got to go. I need...' she stopped. She couldn't even think what it was she needed. 'Do you know where I might find a policeman?'

'Why?' asked the woman. 'What's happened?'

'Please,' said Nancy. 'Can you help?'

'Follow me,' said the woman. 'My name's Miss Thomson. Jean. I'm with the Women Police Volunteers. I'll help you if I can.'

'Oh, thank you, thank you,' said Nancy. 'I'm Nancy Caird, Miss Thomson. Um. What are Women Police Volunteers?'

'I am,' said Jean, her long strides eating up the pavement. Nancy had to scamper to keep up. 'I'm a woman. I volunteer. For the police. It's not really a difficult concept.'

'No, I'm sorry, I see that,' said Nancy. 'I just didn't know there was such a thing. I didn't know women were

97

allowed to help the police.'

'And why *shouldn't* we?' snapped Jean. 'Is there some reason you don't think I should be allowed?'

'Of course not,' said Nancy quickly, afraid that she'd offended the woman. 'I think it's wonderful. I'd like to be a police officer one day.'

'Hmph,' said Jean, apparently mollified. 'Well, that might be taking things too far. They don't even let us vote, you know.'

'They don't?' said Nancy. Nancy didn't know much about politics or voting. She'd been just a small child in 1910, five years before, when the last general election had been held. There had been an election due in 1915, but of course that had been postponed because of the war.

Jean shook her head. 'I worked with the suffragette movement in Dundee, before the war broke out. But now we're at war—' she sighed. 'I changed my strategy. If I couldn't *demand* the vote, why, then, shouldn't I *prove* my value instead? With so many men away at war, there was a need for people in so many areas. I chose to volunteer to help with the police.'

'That's amazing,' said Nancy.

'They don't let me do any real police work. It's mostly welfare I deal with. I was sent up from Dundee tonight to help with the ambulance train. I've spent the last hour chasing up stragglers and taking bottles of whisky off grown men who should know better.' She looked down at Nancy. 'You listen to me, girl. They'll put obstacles in your path. They'll deny you the opportunity to prove yourself. But if you keep at it, keep putting yourself in their faces until they're sick of the sight of you, they'll give in eventually. It's the natural order of things. Women were meant to stand with men, shoulder to shoulder, as equals. And one day we shall. It may take a decade, or it may take a hundred years, but the day is coming.'

Nancy got the feeling that Jean had made this very speech more than once before, but it struck a chord with her.

'Here we are,' said Jean. 'The police station.'

'Aren't you coming in with me?' asked Nancy. She felt suddenly nervous. She got the feeling that Jean wouldn't discount what she had to say just because she was a girl. Jean was used to being ignored because she was a woman. Surely she'd be a more sympathetic ear than a tired desk sergeant?

Jean shook her head. 'I have to be getting back to Dundee,' she said. 'The morning train will be coming through soon.'

'Thank you,' said Nancy. On an impulse she stuck out her hand, as she'd seen her father do to his friends. Jean smiled and shook it.

'Good luck,' said Jean.

'You too,' said Nancy, and she meant it. If Jean could

blaze a trail, by the time Nancy was grown up there might be a clear path to her having a career in the police—or anything else she wanted to be.

The desk sergeant looked as unsympathetic as Nancy had feared. He was piggy-eyed and jowly, and a grumpy expression flicked across his face as soon as he saw Nancy come through the doors. He ostentatiously put his newspaper down on the desk and waited expectantly.

Nancy stopped in her tracks. How on earth was she going to convince him? What evidence did she have? It was a matter of her word, and what was she? A silly little girl who should be home in bed, not running around the streets of Arbroath.

Nancy took a deep breath and tried to channel the spirit of Jean. She took a purposeful step forward and looked up at the desk sergeant.

'Excuse me,' she said, her voice squeakier than she'd intended.

The desk sergeant scowled at her and said nothing.

'I, um, I mean,' began Nancy.

'Spit it out,' snapped the desk sergeant.

'I'm sorry, I just,' tried Nancy, but the forbidding glare of the policeman was too much for her, and she couldn't get the words out. If only Jean had stayed with her!

'Nancy?' came a voice from behind, and Nancy

turned to see Hector and Lachlan sitting on a bench just inside the door. 'What's the matter, lass?'

CHAPTER SIXTEEN
HMS ARGYLL

The captain had assembled the crew on the deck of the *Argyll*. Harry knew that making the call to abandon ship was never an easy one, particularly for a captain, but there was no realistic possibility of making the ship safe to sail again. What was worse, if the *Argyll* was still stuck on the reef by the time the sun came up, it would only be a matter of time before a German submarine spotted them.

The stationary bulk of the *Argyll* would make excellent target practice for a submarine's torpedoes. It would be like shooting fish in a barrel.

Their only consolation was that the storm and the darkness were keeping them hidden. There was no way that a German submarine would be able to see them from any distance. And it was a big sea. The chances of a submarine coming close enough to spot them were tiny. Until the sun came up, of course.

There had been no response to their distress signal.

They had to hope that the message had got through, and that help was on its way. There didn't seem to be much of an alternative. The ship didn't have enough lifeboats for the whole crew—not by some margin—so they were reliant on being rescued by another vessel.

Except—

Harry stared at the lighthouse, the pillar bone-white and spectral through the rain and spray. Harry had the inklings of an idea.

'Sir,' said Harry above the howl of the wind, 'do you think we might be able to contact the lighthouse? If we can get their attention and run a line over to the tower, we might be able to get some of the men off the ship and into the lighthouse.'

The captain pondered for a moment. 'I'm not convinced the tower will hold all that many people,' he said. 'A lighthouse has a crew of three, if I'm not mistaken, and we have six hundred and fifty-five souls on board this ship.'

'It's worth a try, though, sir?'

The captain sighed. 'Go ahead, Mr. Melville,' he said. 'Make your best effort.'

Harry unpacked a loud-hailer from a locker and shouted into it. 'Halloo!' he called. 'Ahoy the lighthouse!' His young voice was swept away into the wind, lost to the storm.

'Give that here,' said a familiar gruff voice, and Chief

Roberts snatched the loud-hailer from Harry's hands and shouted into it. His bellowing voice was five times as loud as Harry's but still the storm swallowed it up. The lighthouse was only a hundred yards away, but there was virtually no chance they'd hear.

'They're probably asleep,' said Dusty Miller.

'How could anyone sleep through this storm?' said Harry.

'By burrowing into your bunk and pulling the blankets over your head,' said Dusty. 'Don't tell me that's not exactly what you'd be doing right now, given the chance.'

Harry grunted. He couldn't remember the last time he'd seen his bunk, and couldn't foresee the next time he'd be enveloped in its comfort. He rummaged through the lockers and brought out two more loud-hailers. He handed them to the most barrel-chested petty officers he could find.

'Keep trying to contact the lighthouse,' he told them. 'Break out the signalling lamp while you're at it. It's one thing to attract their attention. We'll need to be able to talk to them, too.' He looked around, deep in thought. 'Dusty, come with me. We're going to try something else.'

Dusty followed Harry to the bow of the ship. 'What are we doing?' he said, grabbing onto the railing as a wave crashed over the ship and swept across the deck.

'Fetch me a lifebuoy,' said Harry. He had opened a

locker and was pulling out a long coil of grass rope—a type of rope that was actually made from the husk of the coconut, and not grass at all. It was a light, strong rope that floated on the surface of the water and was ideal for rescues. 'We're going to try floating a grass line over to the lighthouse.'

'What good will that do?' asked Dusty. He looked sceptical.

'You never know,' said Harry. 'They might not be able to see a big grey warship in this weather, but a bright red lifebuoy is something else. Or maybe we can get it snagged good and tight on the rocks, and one of us can use it to swim over to the lighthouse.'

'It'll never work,' said Dusty. 'And I'm certainly not volunteering to swim across in these seas.'

'There's a distinct possibility it won't work,' said Harry. 'But I want you to get some crew and try. Keep the men busy. I'm going to try something else.'

He left Dusty standing slack-jawed in the bow, but before he'd gone a dozen paces he could hear the young midshipman barking orders to the crew. Harry climbed the ladder up to the bridge, then carried on to the area of deck in front of the bridge, just below its windows, where the *Argyll*'s 36-inch searchlight was located. He threw the huge switch, and with a noise like a gunshot the searchlight lanced out a beam of radiance right at the lighthouse. Harry played the light over the windows, hoping that the keepers would see their quarters being flooded with light even through the heaviest curtains or the thickest blanket pulled over their heads. Even if they had heavy wooden shutters, Harry hoped the light through the cracks would be bright enough to catch their attention.

'Melville!' shouted Lieutenant Williams. 'For God's sake, man, what are you doing?' The lieutenant reached over and cut off the power to the searchlight.

'Sir, I'm attempting to contact the lighthouse,' said Harry. 'The captain said I could try.'

'That's as may be, but I'm pretty sure the captain never thought that you'd be so stupid as to give away our position to every enemy submarine in the North Sea.'

'I,' began Harry. 'Um. I'm sorry, sir,' he said. 'I didn't realise.' He looked wistfully at the searchlight. He'd been sure his plan would work.

'Get back to the captain. He wants to see you in his cabin,' said the lieutenant.

'He wants to see me? What for?' asked Harry.

'How would I know? Get yourself down there straight away,' said the lieutenant. 'And don't signal any German submarines on your way.'

CHAPTER SEVENTEEN
ARBROATH SIGNAL TOWER

Jamie felt Uncle Stuart's left arm around his neck grow tighter and tighter. He could still feel the impression of the cold steel of the pistol on his head, even though Uncle Stuart had lowered the weapon. The feeling of that gun against his head wasn't one that was going to leave him any time soon. It felt like the barrel had left an indentation in his skin, and an indelible impression. Jamie longed to rub the spot where the gun had been, but every time he moved an arm so much as an inch, Uncle Stuart's grip around his neck tightened.

It was time to admit that he'd got himself into a situation he couldn't get out of. Why had he been so stupid? Why hadn't he just waited outside until Nancy came back with some help? It was all Nancy's fault. He'd never have got into this stupid situation if it hadn't been for her. No, that wasn't fair. She hadn't forced him to come along. But still. It was at least *partly* her fault. Jamie hoped he'd have the opportunity to complain to her.

Mr. Simpson had found the signal lamp and was looking at it like it was a Chinese puzzle. 'How does this thing work, then?' he asked the Master of the Tender, still tied up in his chair.

'Oh, that's easy,' said the Master. 'Hold it by the handle. Now turn it around, sideways.' Mr. Simpson followed his instructions. 'Then take a firm grip in both hands,' Mr. Simpson did so, 'then you shove it RIGHT UP—'

Mr. Simpson slapped the Master with the back of his hand, drawing blood from his lip. The Master licked the blood from his lip and chuckled to himself.

'I don't have time for this nonsense,' said Uncle Stuart. 'Come and hold onto this boy, Simpson. I'll deal with the lamp.' He glanced at the clock on the wall. It was past five in the morning. 'The submarine will be at the mouth of the Tay soon. That's our only chance to signal them the position of the *Argyll*.'

'What's so important about this ship, anyway?' asked Mr. Simpson.

'All I know is, they're carrying something important.' He glanced anxiously over at Jamie, and continued in a whisper. 'We let the submarine know where the ship is, and they'll do the rest.'

'What do you mean, the rest?'

Jamie leaned in closer. He could barely make out what they were saying, but he needed to hear what was going on.

'I don't know. Torpedo it, board it, whatever it takes to get their hands on the cargo.' Uncle Stuart shrugged. 'That's how this game works. Someone else can worry about the whys and wherefores. You just do as you're told, do your bit, keep your mouth shut, and you'll get your reward.'

Mr. Simpson nodded. 'All right,' he said. 'But I still think we should have used the radio.'

'I told you,' said Uncle Stuart, 'the radio is compromised. There are probably police waiting there.'

'I suppose so,' said Mr. Simpson.

'Now grab this little brat,' said Uncle Stuart. 'Don't be afraid to hurt him if you have to.'

'Now come on,' said Mr. Simpson. 'There's no need to be hurting children.'

'There are sailors on board that ship not much older than this boy here,' said Uncle Stuart. 'You're not so worried about them.'

'That's different,' said Mr. Simpson. 'That's war.'

'So is this,' snapped Uncle Stuart, pushing Jamie at the other man. Mr. Simpson put an arm around Jamie's neck. 'Hold still, and he won't hurt you,' said Uncle Stuart, putting his pistol on the table next to the signal lamp. 'Where's the battery?' he asked.

'Battery?' asked Mr. Simpson.

'This wire here. It's supposed to connect to a battery. It's not a complicated bit of equipment, Simpson.

Connect the wire to the battery. Use the sight attached to the top to help aim the beam. Use this trigger to send the signal.'

'I couldn't—'

'You couldn't get it to work because *it wasn't plugged in*,' snapped Uncle Stuart. 'Where did you find the lamp?'

'Over there, in that locker,' said Mr. Simpson.

'And what do we have here?' asked Uncle Stuart, opening the locker. 'Why, it's a battery! Who'd have thought? You really are an idiot, Simpson.'

'Now, steady on,' said Mr. Simpson.

'No, really, you are. And they let you teach schoolchildren?'

'Just shut your mouth, Caird,' said Mr. Simpson.

Jamie noticed that Mr. Simpson's grip around his neck was getting weaker. Maybe this would be his opportunity. With Uncle Stuart concentrating on the signal lamp, and Mr. Simpson distracted by the argument, he might just have a chance to make a break for it.

Out of the corner of his eye, Jamie noticed movement coming from the stairs. Someone was coming up the tower.

'So what's your reward, then, Mr. Simpson?' asked Jamie, as loudly as he could. 'Mr. Caird over there with the pistol said that you'd get your reward. Who's going to give you a reward? What sort of reward do you get for sinking a British ship?'

'Be quiet,' said Mr. Simpson, frowning. The boy was speaking in such a strange, stilted, way. What was he up to?

'Aha!' said Uncle Stuart, who wasn't listening to Jamie. 'Got it!' He flicked the signalling trigger and a bright flash filled the room. 'This'll do the trick.'

Jamie felt Mr. Simpson's arm loosen a fraction more, distracted by the signal lamp, and took his chance. He bit down hard on the flesh on the inside of Mr. Simpson's elbow, his sharp teeth digging through the thin material of Mr. Simpson's jacket and shirt. Jamie's teeth caught flesh. The man screamed with pain, and Jamie dropped to the floor. Two soldiers—the soldiers from the train!— came up the stairs, their rifles at the ready with bayonets glinting evilly on the barrels.

'Hands up!' shouted Hector, his rifle barrel wobbling alarmingly as he tried to keep it steady in his good arm.

Uncle Stuart made a move for the pistol he'd put on the table, but Lachlan took a step forward and aimed his rifle squarely at the man's heart. From that distance, he couldn't possibly miss. Uncle Stuart raised his arms above his head, the signalling lamp still dangling from one hand.

'Now what's all this?' he said, in his most reasonable voice.

'Keep quiet,' said Hector, trying to keep his rifle trained on Mr. Simpson. 'We know exactly what you're up to.'

'My dear fellow,' said Uncle Stuart, 'there seems to have been a terrible misunderstanding. I'm not sure what you think is going on, but if you'll just let me explain—'

'You can explain to me,' said Nancy, coming up the stairs to stand between the soldiers.

Uncle Stuart's mouth hung open. He started to say something, but no words would come out.

The game was up.

CHAPTER EIGHTEEN
HMS ARGYLL

Harry wiped the crusted sea spray from his eyes, tugged at his rain-sodden uniform, and ran his fingers fruitlessly through hair that had turned coarse and matted like seaweed. He'd never pass inspection like this. Still, he doubted anyone else on board looked much better. He rapped on the hatch of the captain's cabin. He was still seething about the lieutenant stopping his attempt with the searchlight, but he'd been in the Royal Navy long enough to understand that the chain of command was sacrosanct, and an order from a superior officer was to be obeyed, no matter how much he disagreed with the decision. That was just the way things were.

It didn't mean he had to like it, though.

'Enter,' said Captain Tancred. The captain was still immaculate in his uniform, with barely a shadow of beard on his chin and not a single button undone or seam out of alignment. Harry was suddenly aware of just how bedraggled he looked from all the running about on deck. He was sure his boots made squelching noises whenever he took a step.

'You wanted to see me, sir?' asked Harry.

'I have a little task for you,' said the captain.

'Sir?'

'I have, in my possession, a dossier that must not fall into enemy hands.'

'Don't worry, sir,' said Harry. 'I'm sure we'll be off the *Argyll* before dawn.'

'I'm sure we will, Mr. Melville, I'm sure we will. But this is what we call contingency planning. Hope for the best, plan for the worst, eh?'

'Yes, sir,' said Harry, wondering what the captain was getting at.

'In the event that we're boarded by the enemy, or the crew is captured, the first thing they'll do is to search my cabin and my person for code books and other documents that we wouldn't want to fall into their hands.'

'How do you know, sir?' asked Harry.

'Because that's what I'd do in their position,' said the captain. 'Intelligence is paramount in modern warfare. Have you read von Clausewitz?'

Harry shook his head. 'No, sir.'

The captain sighed. 'They really should teach this stuff at Dartmouth. Carl von Clausewitz said that in war, intelligence reports tend to be contradictory, false, or uncertain. How much of an advantage, therefore, would it be to rip the intelligence that your enemy is actually *using* right from their hands?' He lifted up a thick folder of papers. 'This is our intelligence.'

'We could destroy it, sir,' said Harry. His signals classes at Naval College had been clear on the importance of destroying code books in the event that the ship was in danger of being boarded. One Royal Navy code book in German hands could change the course of the whole war.

The captain shook his head. 'I've been charged with delivering this dossier to Admiral Jellicoe. Nothing short of imminent danger would be considered an excuse for failing in that endeavour, and I fear that with imminent danger would come a lack of opportunity to do the job satisfactorily.' He handed the dossier to Harry, who took it with trembling hands. 'They can't find this in my cabin or on my person. You're an officer, Mr. Melville, and you've shown on this voyage that you can be trusted.' The captain smiled. 'But no-one would ever think that a lowly middy had been entrusted with such an important package, so it should buy us some time.' He put his hands on Harry's shoulders. 'Do you understand?'

'Yes, sir, I think so,' said Harry.

'Strap it on under your jacket,' said the captain. 'Now, I'm giving you two direct orders. First, and most importantly, keep that dossier out of enemy hands. Second, deliver the dossier to Admiral Jellicoe at Rosyth.

These orders override all other considerations, including your own safety, the safety of the crew, and the safety of the ship.'

'Sir?'

'This is now your top priority, Mr. Melville. Many lives depend on this dossier—many more than just the lives on the *Argyll*.'

'I understand, sir,' said Harry. It was a hard order the captain had given him. For Harry, the ship *was* the Royal Navy. It was the navy world in microcosm, and when you were isolated from the rest of the fleet, it was sometimes difficult to keep in mind that the wider navy existed. Harry had already formed an attachment to the *Argyll* and her crew, so his first instinct was to do everything in his power to keep the ship and the sailors safe.

Harry took off his jacket and the captain helped him to use a large roll of white bandages to wrap the dossier tightly against his stomach. He then put his jacket back on and smoothed out its creases.

'There,' said the captain. 'You'd hardly know you were carrying anything.'

'Yes, sir,' said Harry, who could feel the weight of the dossier in a way that was far more than physical. The paper couldn't be more than a few ounces, but Harry felt weighed down by the extra responsibility that the captain had given him.

'Now,' said the captain, 'let's go and make arrangements

for abandoning ship.'

'I've been trying to contact the lighthouse, but with no luck,' said Harry. 'And there's no sign of any help from shore.'

'Then it's time to deploy the lifeboats,' said the captain.

'We've barely got enough capacity for a hundred or so crew, even packing them in like sardines,' said Harry. 'That will leave more than five hundred still on board ship.'

'I know,' said the captain. 'I'll stay with the ship, of course. But you'll be on the first lifeboat.'

'Sir? No! I can't—'

'Mr. Melville. Haven't you been listening to a word I've been saying?'

'Please don't ask me to do this, sir. Please don't ask me to abandon my shipmates.'

'I'm not asking, Mr. Melville. I'm giving you an order. Do you understand?'

'Yes, sir.'

'Good. Now let's get up on deck and swing out the lifeboats. I don't intend to launch them right away, but I won't be caught napping if anything goes wrong. The lifeboats need to be ready to launch at a moment's notice, and you need to be on hand to make sure that you're on board when they do.'

'Aye aye, captain,' said Harry. Never before had the thought of obeying an order felt so wrong. Never before had he realised that there might be a conflict between his duty and what he knew was right.

CHAPTER NINETEEN
ARBROATH SIGNAL TOWER

'Nancy,' said Uncle Stuart.

'What?' exclaimed Mr. Simpson. 'You know this girl?'

'She's my niece.'

'But—' began Mr. Simpson.

'Don't you recognise me, Mr. Simpson?' asked Nancy. The teacher peered at his pupil. Nancy saw the realisation dawn in Mr. Simpson's eyes.

'You—'

'It's no good,' said Uncle Stuart. 'She knows everything. It's over, Simpson.'

Nancy could see the panic rising in Mr. Simpson. 'No,' he said. 'No. No.'

'They'll hang you,' said the Master of the Tender, still tied up in his chair. 'They'll hang you for the traitor you are.'

'No,' repeated Mr. Simpson. With a panicked leap, he reached for the pistol Uncle Stuart had left lying on the table. His hand was still a foot away from the pistol when the loudest sound Nancy had ever heard cracked across the room, and Mr. Simpson slumped silently to the floor. A tiny curl of smoke spiralled up from the muzzle of Hector's rifle, its barrel suddenly rock-steady in Hector's one good arm.

'Just the one shot,' said Hector quietly, so quietly that Nancy could hardly hear him above the ringing in her ears. 'I had to make it count. I couldn't work the bolt with just one arm. I just had one shot.'

'It's all right, Hector,' said Lachlan, keeping his rifle trained on Uncle Stuart, but looking at his friend out of the corner of one eye. 'You had no choice. He might have hurt the children.'

'Just one shot,' repeated Hector.

'What's the matter with him?' asked Uncle Stuart.

'Not that it's any of your business, but Hector's never shot a man before.' Lachlan glowered at Uncle Stuart. 'It's a hard thing, taking a man's life. You wouldn't understand that, with your plots and plans and submarines and death out of sight. You'd have happily killed a thousand men tonight if you'd sent your signal, and not lost a moment's sleep, I'd wager. But me and Hector, we're made of different stuff.' He lifted his rifle's barrel so it was pointed at Uncle Stuart's head. 'But before you start thinking that I'm a soft touch, let me just tell you this: it wouldn't be the first time *I've* killed a man, and I've got enough ghosts haunting my sleep that one more wouldn't make any difference.'

Uncle Stuart seemed to turn pale.

'Jamie! Are you all right?' asked Nancy, suddenly noticing Jamie lying on the floor.

'I'm fine,' said Jamie. 'I'm not hurt.'

'I was worried when I couldn't find you outside. Why didn't you wait for me like I told you to?'

'You're not my boss, Nancy Caird,' said Jamie. 'I don't have to do everything you tell me. And if I hadn't distracted them when I saw you coming up the stairs, who knows what would have happened?'

'I suppose so,' said Nancy.

Jamie got to his feet and picked up Uncle Stuart's pistol from the table.

'Here, lad, be careful. Give that here,' said Lachlan, taking the pistol from Jamie's hand. He let his rifle hang down by its strap and pointed the pistol at Uncle Stuart.

'Why, Uncle Stuart? Why did you do it?' asked Nancy.

'Why does anyone do anything?' said Uncle Stuart tiredly. 'Take your good friend Simpson there. Did you know his wife was German? She was looking after her sickly father in Germany when the war began. One of the Kaiser's spies discovered their relationship and decided to use her as leverage against the poor fool. He thought that if he did as he was told, he'd get to see her again one day.' He shook his head. 'He never was very bright.'

'That's all well and good,' said Jamie as he untied the

Master of the Tender. 'But you don't have a German wife, do you?'

Uncle Stuart shook his head. 'No. No, I don't.'

'If you'll excuse me,' said the Master, 'I'll go and make a couple of telephone calls. There's a ship on the rocks, and I need to call out the lifeboats. I'll be down at the lifeboat station if you need me.' He paused. 'You might want to take this one in to the police.' He headed off down the stairs.

Jamie helped Hector to sit in the vacated chair. The wounded soldier seemed cold and distant, and Jamie hoped that he'd be all right. He can't have expected to come home to Scotland from the horrors of the trenches and still end up having to take a man's life. He must have thought that he'd already given enough to the war. War had a habit of taking more and more from you, long after you thought it had taken everything. Or so it seemed to Jamie. He placed a hand on the man's shoulder and hoped that it was comforting.

'So what's your excuse, Uncle Stuart? Why did you become a traitor?' asked Nancy.

'Now, Nancy, that's a very harsh word, traitor,' said Uncle Stuart. 'It never started that way. It was back in 1910, and I was in Calais arranging a shipment of spices and silks for the London market. I was duped, not for the first time, and I lost the shipment and all of my money— including money I'd borrowed from some dubious

Parisians. The sort of people who don't take kindly to late payments. A young man from Germany heard of my plight and offered me a way out of my predicament. All I had to do was write a few letters to him with details of shipping passing in and out of the various ports I visited, and he'd settle my debts and provide me with a small stipend. I mean, what was the harm? At first I assumed he was in the shipping business, and was looking to gain some sort of competitive advantage over his rivals, but over the next few months he began asking more and more about navy ships. I confronted him, and he admitted he worked for the Imperial German Navy. But still, what was the harm? These weren't secrets I was telling him. Anyone with eyes could see the ships sail in and out of the harbour.'

'But he was German,' said Nancy.

'What difference did that make? Half the business deals I made were with German companies. We weren't at war. We weren't even on unfriendly terms. What possible harm could it cause?' Uncle Stuart sighed. 'Then the tensions between Germany and Britain started to grow. I sent a letter to my contact and told him, very clearly, that I wouldn't be able to send him any more information. He turned up at my offices one evening, completely unannounced, and explained to me, very patiently, that I'd already nailed my colours to the mast of *Nachrichten Abteilung im Admiralstab*.'

'The what?' asked Jamie.

'German Naval Intelligence. Even the Germans with their love of long words tend to abbreviate it to simply *N*. He meant, of course, that if I stopped providing information, all he had to do was leak to British Intelligence that I'd been spying for *N*, and I'd be in prison before I knew it.'

'You could have refused. You could have come clean,' said Nancy.

'I could have,' said Uncle Stuart. 'But they also offered me a lot more money, now the nature of the business was out in the open. I hadn't had any more luck with my various businesses, and the situation in Europe was making importing and exporting fraught with complications.' He shrugged. 'It was easy money. Until they paired me with Simpson there.' He gestured to the body on the floor. 'He'd been sending radio signals to German submarines for months, providing details of the ships sailing up and down the Tay, but he'd become erratic. I was supposed to keep him on the straight and narrow. Remind him of what he was doing all this for. A few days ago I passed on a message from his wife. He got quite agitated, and I had to lay down the law.'

'That must have been what I heard,' said Nancy.

'I suppose it must. On such chances and trifles do great schemes flounder,' said Uncle Stuart. 'Ah well.

I suppose there's nothing to be done.' He yawned and stretched out his arms.

'Here, you,' said Lachlan, 'stay still.' The soldier was suddenly aware that the man had been moving slowly, almost imperceptibly, towards the table. What was he up to?

'Why?' asked Uncle Stuart. 'You have my pistol. There's nothing I can do to escape.' He placed his palms on the table and leaned forward. 'It's all over for me. If I'm to face a firing squad, so be it.'

'I don't know how you can be so—' began Nancy, as Uncle Stuart grabbed the handle of the signalling lamp and blasted it right in Lachlan's face, blinding him. With a grunt of effort, Uncle Stuart flipped the table, knocking it into Hector and Jamie, then rushed down the stairs before anyone could stop him.

'After him!' shouted Jamie, untangling himself from the upturned chair and running down the stairs, but before he reached the bottom he heard the sound of a motor car starting up. By the time he reached the door, the car was already speeding down the road.

Uncle Stuart had escaped.

CHAPTER TWENTY
BELL ROCK LIGHTHOUSE

Assistant Keeper Donald MacDonald stretched, yawned, and put down his mug of tea. The Bell Rock Lighthouse's kitchen was the heart of the tower, the warmest room of the whole structure, but he could hear the storm howling outside and the roar of the surf beating against the rocks below. He could feel the whole tower sway in the wind, bending but not breaking, which was just as her engineers had intended, but still, it was a disconcerting feeling. He knew that as soon as he moved from the kitchen the cold would nip at his face and his fingers, but he couldn't put it off any longer. He had his duty to do, after all.

'Time to switch the light on,' he said, regretfully, checking his pocket watch against the mantel clock. While the lighthouse was kept dark most of the time, there was a schedule to display the signal at fixed times, just for short periods, and it was coming up to the early morning lighting-up time.

Principal Keeper John Henderson nodded. 'Get yourself up that tower, then,' he said. 'I'll brew up another pot of tea. Is it too early for breakfast, do you think?'

'Oh no,' said MacDonald. 'I could manage a wee spot of breakfast. Go and wake up Colin. It's his turn to cook.' The second Assistant Keeper Colin McCormack was still in bed—he'd had the late watch. Not that the lightkeepers had been doing much in the way of keeping watch. The storm had been too fierce to risk opening any of the doors or windows, and with no light to maintain or mechanism to keep wound, their watches had been mostly concerned with keeping the tea pot full. Which was, after all, an extremely important task.

'I'll get Colin started on the breakfast if you get up that tower. Check the signal at the shore station, too.'

MacDonald nodded. When they lit the lamp in the early morning, the shore station would respond by raising their 18-inch copper signalling ball up the mast on top of the tower. Through a telescope, the signal was clearly visible, and it meant that all was well. However, if the shore station didn't raise the signal, that meant that something was amiss, and there would be a signal coming by signalling lamp—the keepers should get a pad and pencil to take down the message. MacDonald really hoped there wouldn't be any messages today. He was already thinking about his breakfast.

He started the climb to the lightroom. At least he

didn't have to climb all the way from the ground floor up the tower—while the Bell Rock Lighthouse was one hundred and sixteen feet tall, the kitchen was only a couple of floors below the balcony level. MacDonald climbed past the bedroom floor where McCormack was sleeping cocooned in a blanket against the chill, past the library floor where they spent much of their days reading and chatting, up to the lightroom. He checked the time, then reached into the lantern, past the powerful lenses, to light the paraffin lamp. He then pulled open the heavy iron door of the revolving machinery and began winding the great lever that pulled the weight up the central shaft of the lighthouse. The clockwork mechanism used the slow descent of the weight back down the central shaft, its motion converted through a series of gears and governors into a slow and steady rotation of the lens array, the lenses gliding smoothly on the bath of mercury. The lamp itself didn't rotate, but the lenses rotated around it, focusing the light into sharp beams that were visible up to thirty miles away. The higher the tower, the less frequently you had to wind the mechanism. On the other hand, the higher the tower, the further you had to climb to get to the lightroom. MacDonald could see advantages and disadvantages in both. He was enjoying his time at the Bell Rock, but sometimes the thought of a nice short tower on terra firma with just a handful of steps appealed to him even more. Particularly when the weather was as bad as it was now. There was an incredible sense of isolation when you were trapped in a tower sticking out of a mostly submerged reef, and while he trusted Stevenson and Rennie, the engineers who had built the tower over a hundred years before, it was disconcerting to hear the building creak and groan in the storm.

He looked out at the rain battering against the glass, sheets of water cascading down the window in the gale, twisting and distorting the view. He didn't fancy going out onto the balcony. He'd heard of a keeper being swept over the railings in weather just like this—although he was never sure whether Henderson was just pulling his leg when he trotted out his stories of accidents, maimings, and mysterious disappearances. What was that tall tale he told about Flannan Isle? All three keepers disappeared without a trace, their meal lying cold on the table, only an overtoppled chair to indicate anything had gone wrong? Pure nonsense!

MacDonald pulled his cap down tight on his head and braced himself to face the elements. It would only take a few seconds to check the shore station through the telescope, then he'd be back in the warmth. He thought about breakfast, and his stomach rumbled. With any luck McCormack would be frying up the bacon right now.

He pulled back the heavy bolt and opened the hatch,

ducking down to climb through out onto the balcony. He gasped as the wind and rain hit him, and grabbed onto his cap as the storm threatened to rip it from his head. He pulled it off and stuck it inside his jacket for safekeeping.

He squinted against the rain and was about to put his eye to the telescope when he saw a huge grey shape through the storm. An enormous warship, bristling with weapons, its guns pointing right at the tower. The Germans had come!

'It's the Germans! It's the Germans!' shouted MacDonald, racing back down to the kitchen. 'They're right on top of us!'

'What are you talking about?' said McCormack sleepily. He'd pulled a jumper on over his pyjamas rather than get dressed properly.

'There's a bloody great ship getting ready to shell us! What do we do?'

'A ship? Where?' asked Henderson.

'Come and see,' said MacDonald. He ran back up to the lantern room, his heavy boots slipping and sliding on the rain-slick deck. A gale blew through the still-open hatch, snatching up papers into a whirlwind, and the whole tower swayed and groaned in protest. Shielding his eyes against the wind and rain, he raised his arm. 'There! Over there! You can't miss it!'

'What do we do?' asked McCormack. 'They can't miss

us at that range. They'll turn us to rubble.' He looked down at the rock below. It was visible only as a roiling mass of churning sea. There was nowhere to go. They had no boat. They had no escape.

Flickering lights appeared on the ship, and a bellowing sound carried across the water.

'What are they waiting for?' asked MacDonald. 'Why don't they just fire?'

'Wait,' said Henderson. 'Look. Listen.'

'What?' asked McCormack.

'Since when did Germans sound like they come from Dundee?'

CHAPTER TWENTY-ONE
HMS ARGYLL

Harry put down the loudhailer and suppressed a yell of joy. They'd been seen! The lightkeepers had finally noticed the eleven thousand ton battleship on their doorstep! It had taken them long enough.

'Signal the keepers!' he shouted to the petty officer with the signal lamp. 'Tell them we need help.'

'Aye aye,' said the petty officer, and began sending a Morse code message with his lamp, his fingers hammering the trigger in rapid time. Before long, the lighthouse was signalling back.

Harry ran to the captain and made his report. 'Sir! We've made contact with the lighthouse at last. The keepers are going to float a line to us.'

'Good. Good,' said the captain in a distracted tone, looking towards the lightening eastern horizon. Even through the storm, the hint of morning was apparent. 'We need to get off the ship before it's properly light.' He sighed. 'We're a sitting duck, Mr. Melville, and I don't mind telling you that it's not a pleasant feeling. If a German submarine had so much as an inkling that we were in the area, we'd be done for.' He stared at Harry. 'I thought I told you to stay by the lifeboats?'

Harry opened his mouth to reply, but nothing he could think of sounded suitable. 'On my way, sir,' he said eventually.

By the time Harry got back to the deck, the lightkeepers had floated a line attached to an empty barrel across to the ship. 'Blimey,' said Harry. 'That works a lot better than trying to use a lifebuoy.' He helped the sailors attach a heavy hawser to the line, then signalled to the lighthouse to haul the rope back across. They'd be able to use the hawser to propel the sailors to the lighthouse, one lifeboat-full at a time. By hauling themselves along the line, they'd avoid getting dashed against the lethal rocks.

'Message,' said a radio operator at Harry's elbow. He'd never get used to the way the radio men appeared out of nowhere and delivered their terse messages. Harry took the slip of paper and read it with mounting excitement.

'Chief Roberts!' he called out to the petty officer paying out the hawser. 'Don't bother with that rope. I've got a message from Rosyth. They sent out lifeboats from Arbroath, Broughty Ferry, and St. Andrews, but they've had to turn back.'

'That doesn't sound like good news, lad,' grumbled the chief.

'Oh, but it is,' said Harry. 'In their place they're sending two destroyers from the night patrol. HMS *Hornet* and HMS *Jackal* are on their way.'

'Now that's more like it!' grinned the chief. 'I didn't fancy huddling in a lighthouse or taking a trip in a lifeboat anyway. I don't feel right unless I've got a proper iron-clad ship beneath my feet.' He waved at his men. 'Haul the rope back, lads! We'll be going to visit some of our Navy brethren instead!' He pulled on the hawser, and his party pulled with him.

'Wait, wait!' called out Harry. He pulled out his binoculars. 'The hawser! It's tripped up one of the keepers!' One of the lightkeepers had been standing at the entrance to the tower, and when the chief and his men pulled back on the rope, it had knocked him off his feet.

'He should know better than to get in the way of a rope,' said the chief, continuing to pull.

'I said STOP!' shouted Harry. Through his binoculars he could see the keeper being pulled towards the lip of the entrance, towards a thirty foot drop onto surging seas and razor sharp rocks. The other two keepers were clinging onto their companion, trying to stop him being pulled to his death.

Harry punched Chief Roberts on the arm, and the

sailor stopped pulling, more in surprise than in pain. Harry's fist had been like a snowflake landing on a brick.

'What was that for?' asked the chief. 'You'd better have a good explanation!'

Harry ignored the sailor and lifted his binoculars again. The slack rope had allowed one of the keepers to cut the hawser wrapped around the keeper's leg, and they were bundling him back inside the tower.

'Sorry about that, Chief,' said Harry. 'They're clear now. You can carry on hauling the rope back.'

'Oh, can I, now?' asked the sailor in a belligerent tone.

'If you would be so kind, Chief,' said Harry. 'I, ah, hope I didn't hurt you.'

The chief looked at Harry for a second, then burst out laughing. 'All right, lad. All right. Heave!' he called out.

Harry leaned in to the petty officer with the signal lamp. 'See if you can signal the lighthouse,' he said. 'Thank the keepers for their help, but tell them we've got ships on the way to rescue us, and they can stand down.'

'Will do,' said the petty officer. He squinted into the storm. 'I don't think they're paying us much attention at the moment, though.'

'Perhaps not,' said Harry. 'I think they might be a little bit occupied with a small accident. But if you get the chance, please pass the message on.'

The petty officer nodded.

Harry pondered his next move. If there were

destroyers on the way to effect a rescue, they wouldn't need the *Argyll*'s lifeboats. Did that mean the captain's orders weren't needed any more?

If there was one thing Harry knew about captain's orders, it was that it was probably not a good idea to decide on your own interpretation. He'd get his instructions right from the horse's mouth.

'Keep an eye on things here,' he told Dusty Miller. 'I'm going to see the captain.'

CHAPTER TWENTY-TWO
ARBROATH

'It's over,' said Jamie.

Hector and Lachlan nodded sadly.

'No,' said Nancy. 'We have to catch him. We have to catch my uncle before he does anything else.'

'What can he do?' asked Jamie. 'We've stopped him signalling the submarine. He can't do any more harm.'

'You're forgetting one thing,' said Nancy.

'What's that?' asked Jamie.

'He still has a radio back in Dundee.'

'But—' began Jamie. 'He wouldn't dare, would he? He thinks there are police watching the office by the docks.'

'I don't know,' said Nancy. 'But he might. And there's a ship out there marooned on the rocks. All it would take is one short message, and a submarine could blow it out of the water.'

'I, uh—' said Jamie.

'The lassie's right,' said Hector quietly. 'We'll go to the police station. We'll tell them everything that's happened.

They'll be able to call ahead to Dundee.'

'All right,' said Nancy, 'let's go. There's no time to waste.'

Hector and Lachlan led the way, with Jamie and Nancy hurrying on after them as best they could. They were on the verge of exhaustion, and Nancy fretted as the two soldiers strode on ahead of them.

'Jamie,' she said.

'Yes?' puffed Jamie.

'What if they don't believe us?'

'It's not just us now,' said Jamie. 'There's Hector and Lachlan, too.'

'But when I met up with them earlier, they were in the police station. I think they were in a spot of trouble. I'm not sure the police will be very happy about them rushing off to help me.'

'Ah,' said Jamie.

'What do we do?'

'We just have to do our best,' said Jamie. 'It's not like we can chase after him to Dundee all by ourselves. For a start, we don't have a car.'

'We wouldn't need a car,' said Nancy. 'The morning train is due any minute.'

Jamie stopped in his tracks. 'Hector! Lachlan!' he called to the men. 'You go on. We're going back to Dundee. We're taking the train.'

'Oh are you, indeed?' said Lachlan. 'Not on your

own, you're not. Hector. You go on to the police station and explain what's happened. I'll go with these two troublemakers and see that they don't get into any more mischief.'

Hector nodded and headed for the police station. He looked as if he was grateful to get some time to spend alone with his thoughts after the events at the shore station.

'So what are you two waiting for?' asked Lachlan. 'The train station's this way.'

Nancy and Jamie hurried after him.

The train was already on the platform by the time they reached the station.

'Hurry!' called out Lachlan, running on ahead.

The station master blew his whistle, and with a cloud of smoke and a hiss of steam, the train started to move.

'We're too late,' said Jamie.

'Just run,' said Nancy. They raced along the platform, and right in front of them a door opened.

'Get in,' said Jean, reaching out a hand to Nancy. The volunteer police woman helped each of them into the carriage, then slammed the door as the train picked up speed and left the station. 'Now what are you up to, Nancy?' She squinted at Lachlan. 'I know you. I picked you up last night, wandering around town with your friend with a bottle in your hands.'

'That was me, all right,' said Lachlan sheepishly.

'But I don't know you,' said Jean to Jamie.

'Jamie Balfour, Miss.'

'He's my friend,' said Nancy. Jamie looked slightly surprised, then nodded as he realised it was true. He'd only known Nancy for a day or so, but they'd been through so much together already.

'So what on earth is going on?' asked Jean.

Nancy filled the volunteer police woman in with all the details, with Jamie chipping in occasionally to clarify things and Lachlan nodding in agreement. Nancy was glad Lachlan was there to back them up.

'Well,' said Jean at last. 'That's quite a story. How do you know he's headed back to Dundee?'

'We don't,' said Jamie. 'But we can't take the chance.'

'I see,' said Jean. 'Well, in that case, I'd better help you, if I can.'

'Oh, would you?' said Nancy.

'Of course,' said Jean. 'And here's Dundee coming up.' The train slowed down and pulled into Dundee West Railway Station.

CHAPTER TWENTY-THREE
HMS ARGYLL

'I told you to stay by the lifeboats!' thundered Captain Tancred.

'Yes, sir,' said Harry, who'd been expecting the bluster. 'But I thought you'd want to know that HMS *Jackal* and HMS *Hornet* are coming to our rescue. I presume this changes my orders, but I wanted to confirm with you.'

'Destroyers, are they?' mused the captain.

'Yes, sir,' said Harry.

'Hmm,' said the captain. 'We won't get two ships alongside the *Argyll*, not in these seas,' he said. 'We can use our lifeboats to transfer at least some of the crew across to one of the destroyers. If it lies off to our starboard, it will shelter us from the worst of the weather, and the lifeboats will have an easier time rowing in her lee. It may take a few trips, but we should be able to get everyone across.'

'Sounds like a good plan, sir,' said Harry.

'Get yourself back to the lifeboats, then,' said the

captain. 'Your orders haven't changed.'

'Aye aye, captain,' said Harry.

'Make sure you signal the *Jackal* and *Hornet* with the plan. Transmit by radio, then back up the message with the signal lamp and semaphore. We've had enough miscommunication today.'

'Aye aye,' said Harry again.

'Dismissed,' said the captain. 'I'll see you on the boat deck.'

'That's the *Jackal*,' shouted Harry to Dusty, pointing to the indistinct grey shape off to the *Argyll*'s starboard.

'She's still some distance off,' said Dusty. 'It'll take ages to row all that way.'

'You'd better signal her to come closer,' agreed Harry. 'We have enough lifeboat space for maybe a hundred. Six or seven round trips are going to take a long time.'

'Middy!' exclaimed a familiar voice, and Harry turned to see Chief Roberts.

'What is it, Chief?' asked Harry.

'You'd better come and see this,' he said.

He led Harry to the stern of the *Argyll*, and pointed to the massive shape of a destroyer slowly moving towards them.

'What are they doing, Chief?' asked Harry.

'We got a signal from Captain Bingham on the

Hornet, said the chief. 'He said they were going to try an approach.'

Harry looked on in horror. The storm was abating slightly, but the seas were still enormous. The *Hornet* was being lifted up then slammed back down by the force of the waves. What on earth was Bingham doing? Harry had transmitted Captain Tancred's orders, and the *Argyll*'s captain was a full captain—while the commander of a destroyer was *called* a captain, he usually didn't hold the *rank* of a captain in the Royal Navy. A destroyer's commander was usually a Lieutenant-Commander or a Commander. Captain Tancred almost certainly outranked the commanders of both the *Hornet* and the *Jackal*.

'It'll never work,' said Harry.

'Oh, I don't know,' said Chief Roberts. 'He might be able to pull it off. See? He's coming in backwards. He's going to line up stern-to-stern. If he gets it right, we should be able to jump across.'

'Sounds crazy,' said Harry.

'That's destroyer captains for you,' said the chief. 'They're all a bit cracked in the head. Comes of being used as an extra layer of armour for our capital ships and being put up against enemy dreadnoughts twenty-five times their size. Makes them a little bit reckless, in my experience.'

The *Hornet* was closing more quickly than Harry

would have liked.

'All right,' said Harry. 'Let's get as many men to the stern as we can. If he *can* pull it off, it'll be a lot quicker than using the lifeboats.'

The chief nodded.

'I'd better tell the captain,' said Harry.

Captain Tancred hadn't been happy with the developments at all. He'd raged at the idiocy of destroyer commanders for several minutes before calming down.

'All right,' he said at last. 'We'll do both. Get as many men into the lifeboats as possible and send them across to the *Jackal*. The rest can try to board the *Hornet*.'

'Which will you take, sir?' asked Harry.

'I'll see the lifeboats off, then join the men at the stern,' said the captain. 'There's no chance that I will leave this ship while there's still a single man left on it. I'd rather stay behind than abandon ship without all my crew.'

'Yes, sir,' said Harry. 'But let's hope it doesn't come to that.'

The boat deck was thronged with sailors readying the lifeboats. They swung out on their booms over the water then were lowered into the sea.

Harry directed the launching of the lifeboats and watched as the last one started moving across the surface of the water towards the *Jackal*.

'Right, sir, let's get you onto the *Hornet*,' said Harry to the captain.

The captain turned to see Harry standing beside him.

'Blast it, Melville, I expected you to be on one of those lifeboats!'

'Sorry, sir,' said Harry. 'There wasn't room on the last one.' Harry had no intention of leaving his captain alone. Captains sometimes had strange ideas about the shame of abandoning their ships, and Harry hadn't liked Captain Tancred's talk about staying behind. Harry felt a wrench at having to leave the *Argyll* behind on this reef, and he'd only been a member of her crew for a few days. How much worse must it be for her captain?

'This way, sir,' said Harry, leading the way to the stern.

Most of the crew had already made it across to the *Hornet*. Her (possibly insane) captain had backed the destroyer right up to the stern of the *Argyll*. Harry could hear the ear-piercing shriek of metal armour plates buckling and crumpling as the *Hornet*'s stern scraped against the bigger ship. The sea was lifting the destroyer up and down like an elevator, while the *Argyll* was motionless on the reef.

'How—' began Harry.

'Timing,' said the captain. 'Watch.'

The crew on the stern waited for the destroyer's stern to rise to the apex of its climb, then jumped from the *Argyll* onto the deck of the smaller ship, where they were grabbed by their shipmates and pulled to safety. Harry swallowed nervously. If he got the timing wrong, the difference in the heights of the ships' decks would mean an awfully long drop.

The last ten of the crew made the jump, all at the same time, and then it was just Harry and the captain on the stern.

'The ship's clear, sir,' said Harry nervously. 'It's time for us to leave, too, I think.'

'Are you ready?' asked the captain.

Harry nodded, but secretly was thinking that he should have taken the lifeboat.

'Then *jump!*' shouted the captain, leaping from the *Argyll's* rail to the destroyer below. Harry froze for a second, then leapt into space. His stomach lurched and he felt for certain that his heart had stopped in-between beats. He saw the captain land and roll on the deck, which then came up to meet him, slowly, more slowly than it should have, and he realised with a sickening sensation that he'd hesitated for too long, and the *Hornet* was already dropping on the wave crest.

He landed with a thump and felt something give in his ankle.

CHAPTER TWENTY-FOUR
DUNDEE

The office where Uncle Stuart and Mr. Simpson had kept their radio was dark. There was no sign of any police, which made Nancy think that Hector mustn't have been able to convince the Arbroath police that they needed to act.

Nancy hoped that Hector was all right. She felt guilty about leaving him on his own when he'd been so shaken up, and knew that Lachlan had to be feeling the same.

'Wait out here,' said Lachlan. 'I'll take a look inside.' He disappeared into the darkness within the building.

'There certainly doesn't seem to be anyone here now,' said Jean.

'Could we have got here before Uncle Stuart?' asked Nancy.

'I wouldn't have thought so,' said Jean. 'Modern trains are very fast, but with a head start, a car would have beaten us by some margin.'

'Perhaps he's been and gone,' said Jamie.

'Perhaps,' said Jean. 'All right. Once Lachlan comes out, we'll go down to the police station and take your statements. Your friend—Hector was it?—back in Arbroath may have some explaining to do, given that there's a dead spy at the shore station, so the sooner we get everything written down, officially, the better for all concerned.'

'I suppose so,' said Nancy. 'I just—' she shook her head. 'I've got the feeling I'm missing something.'

'Where is Lachlan?' said Jamie. 'He's taking a while.'

Right on cue, Lachlan's face appeared at the window. 'There's nobody here,' he shouted through the glass. 'The radio valves are cold, too. Does anyone know how to disable a radio, just in case? I don't just want to smash it,' he said.

'Wait there,' said Jean. 'I'll be with you in a second.'

As Jean entered the building, Jamie looked at Nancy. 'I don't fancy going down the police station and giving statements,' he said.

'Me neither,' she replied. 'And anyway, I've been thinking. What if he wasn't coming here? What if Uncle Stuart was heading for somewhere else?'

'He could be anywhere,' said Jamie. 'He'll have disappeared by now.'

'But if you're going to disappear, you need money, don't you?' said Nancy. 'And you heard him back at the shore station. He did all this for the money.'

'What are you getting at?' asked Jamie.

'Back at his house, I saw him open his safe. There was a lot of money in there. Bundles and bundles of banknotes.'

'Hmmm,' said Jamie. 'He wouldn't want to leave that behind.'

'No,' said Nancy. 'No, I don't think he would.'

'Right,' said Jamie. 'Before the grown-ups come back and drag us off to the police station. Let's go check out your uncle's house.'

There was a light in the window of Uncle Stuart's house, but Nancy couldn't remember if she'd left the light on when she climbed through the window all those hours ago. Hours? It felt like days!

'Look,' said Jamie, pointing to the front door. It was standing slightly ajar. 'It wasn't like that when we left,' he said. 'Or I wouldn't have bothered smashing the window to get you out.'

Nancy pushed the door gently and cringed as it creaked softly on its old hinges.

'Shh!' hissed Jamie.

'I'm *trying* to be quiet,' whispered Nancy.

Nancy saw her coat still hanging in the hallway, and was suddenly aware of how cold and wet she was. She'd missed that coat. She lifted it down from the hook and put it on.

'What are you doing?' asked Jamie, as quietly as he could.

'I'm cold,' said Nancy matter-of-factly.

The door to the study was open, the key still in its keyhole, and they could see the light from its lamps dappling the hall carpet. Nancy crept to the doorway, and looked inside.

Uncle Stuart was there, crouched down over the safe.

'Damn and blast!' he said to himself, brushing away shards and slivers of glass from the broken window. He knelt on the cleared carpet and unlocked the safe. He pulled the wad of banknotes out and stuffed the cash into his inside jacket pocket.

'Have you found what you're looking for, Uncle?' asked Nancy loudly.

'What?' Uncle Stuart leapt to his feet.

'The money. That's what's important to you, isn't it?'

'You don't understand,' said Uncle Stuart. 'It's not the money that's important. It's what it can buy me. And it can buy me freedom. Freedom from blasted *N* and their spies. Freedom from the police. Freedom from *everything*.'

'I don't think you've got enough money for that,' said Jamie, coming to stand beside Nancy.

'No, you may be right,' said Uncle Stuart. 'But it's a start. Look,' he said, spreading his hands wide, 'this doesn't need to get any uglier than it already has.'

'I saw a man die tonight,' said Nancy.

'And I saw a man have to kill,' said Jamie.

'I don't want to hurt you. Either of you,' said Uncle Stuart.

Jamie strode to the fireplace and picked up a wicked-looking iron poker. He had no intention of letting the man hurt Nancy.

'Then it's simple,' said Nancy. 'Turn yourself in.'

Uncle Stuart laughed. 'No, Nancy, I don't think so. I'm going to walk out of that door, get into the car, and drive off. You'll never see me again. I'll never work for *N* again. That's not so bad, is it? What good would it do, putting me behind bars? Or worse! They could put me in front of a firing squad. Is that what you want for your old uncle, Schatzi?'

Nancy flinched. He'd used the pet name he'd always called her. The *German* pet name. *Schatzi*. Treasure. Like gold and jewels and money. The only thing Uncle Stuart cared about. It was exactly the wrong word to use. She'd been starting to soften in her resolve, but that one word, that one little ridiculous word, changed everything.

'Jamie,' she said. 'Come here.'

Jamie looked at her standing by the doorway. Holding his poker like a sword, and keeping an eye on Uncle Stuart, he backed towards the door.

'You were always my favourite uncle,' she said.

'That's good, Nancy,' said Uncle Stuart.

'But I can't let you go.' Pulling Jamie by the arm, she stepped into the hallway, slammed the door shut, and turned the key in the lock.

CHAPTER TWENTY-FIVE
ROSYTH

Harry rubbed the bandage on his ankle and grimaced with the pain.

'Here, lad, have some tea,' said Chief Roberts, handing Harry a steaming hot mug. He leaned in, and in a conspiratorial whisper added, 'The canteen ladies might have slipped a little something extra in there.'

Harry took a sip and winced. A *little* something? The mug was more rum than tea! 'Thanks, Chief,' said Harry, looking around the Rosyth mess. He was warm, he was dry, he had a hot mug in his hands, and the events of the last day seemed so distant that he almost thought he'd dreamed them. 'Have you seen the captain?' he asked.

The chief shook his head. 'I think he's with the top brass. Explaining how he managed to sail right into a lighthouse.'

'That's not fair,' said Harry. 'We had no way of knowing the light wasn't on.'

The chief shrugged. 'That's true enough,' he said,

'but that's not how this works. A warship has been lost, without enemy action, so someone has to take the blame.'

'How about blaming Rosyth command for not passing on our message to the lighthouse?' said Harry.

'Quiet, lad,' said the chief. 'You won't do yourself any favours blaming command.' He looked up. 'Speak of the devil,' he said, gesturing to the doorway of the mess. Captain Tancred was coming in, leading enough top brass to provide the ballast for a dreadnought. 'That's Admiral Jellicoe there, right behind the captain.'

The captain waved Harry over.

With a grunt he got to his feet, picked up his things, and gingerly hobbled over to where the captain stood with the senior officers. He attempted his best parade salute.

'This is the midshipman I was telling you about,' said the captain.

'Mr. Melville, is it?' said the admiral.

'Yes, sir,' said Harry.

'Trustworthy, you say?' said the admiral to Captain Tancred.

'Yes, sir. He kept your documents safe and secret until I relieved him of them here in Rosyth.'

'Good, good,' said the admiral. He looked at Harry's ankle. 'Injured in battle, Mr. Melville?'

'Not quite, sir,' said Harry.

'I'm afraid Mr. Melville took a tumble when we

jumped to the *Hornet*,' said the captain.

'Ah,' said the admiral. 'Never mind. I'm sure you'll find your sea legs someday.'

Harry bristled but knew better than to respond to that remark with anything other than 'Yes, sir.'

'As your captain has been so careless with his vessel, we're going to have to find new postings for you all.'

'That's not quite fair, sir,' said Harry, and then suddenly wished he'd kept his mouth shut.

'Oh?' said the admiral.

'Please excuse Mr. Melville, sir,' said the captain. 'He was only on the *Argyll* for a short time, but he was very fond of her. And loyalty to your captain is hardly the worst vice a middy can have.'

'I suppose not,' said the admiral. 'If you can control your outspoken impulses, Mr. Melville, we may have an assignment for you. We've been looking for someone loyal and trustworthy and not entirely stupid, and James here seems to think you fit the bill.' He looked over Harry one more time. 'We'll be in touch,' he said.

The admiral and the rest of the officers left, leaving Harry with the captain.

'What was all that about, sir?' asked Harry.

The captain sighed. 'They've been looking for someone to punish,' he said. 'Old Jellicoe started sniffing around you, as you were on watch when we hit the rock, you were carrying the dossier, and you were the last to leave the ship.'

'But—' said Harry.

'I know. The accident had nothing to do with you. But being in the wrong place at the wrong time can be fatal to a man's career. I had to exaggerate your position on the *Argyll*. I had to tell them you were involved throughout the affair not through chance, but because I'd taken you under my wing as the most promising of the midshipmen.' He sighed. 'Unfortunately it seems that I've been a bit too effusive in my praise, and the admiral now has you pegged for one of his pet projects.'

'You shouldn't have done that, sir,' said Harry. 'What if they blame you instead?'

'Ah, Mr. Melville. Do you think they'll ever give me another command after I've run one of Jellicoe's ships into a reef?'

'But—'

'I know. It's not fair. I'll be sailing a desk for the rest of my career.' He shook his head. 'But at least you might have a future in the Royal Navy. If you can survive the admiral's project.'

'Have you any idea what it is, sir?' asked Harry. He didn't want to be involved in a pet project. He wanted to be on board a warship. He wanted to prove himself and work up through the ranks until he was given a command of his own.

The captain shrugged. 'It's something to do with the

Naval Intelligence Division. That's all I know.' He looked Harry in the eye. 'I'm afraid I might have dropped you right in it,' he said.

'Wrong place at the wrong time, sir,' said Harry with a rueful grin.

CHAPTER TWENTY-SIX
DUNDEE

Jean placed the tray filled with mugs of cocoa down on the table. 'Drink up,' she said. 'Before it gets cold.'

'Thank you,' said Nancy, picking up her mug. Jamie nodded his thanks.

The door to the interview room opened. 'Jean,' said the desk sergeant. 'Your other guests are here.'

'Hector! Lachlan!' exclaimed Nancy, leaping to her feet and giving them both big hugs.

'I'll get more cocoa,' said Jean.

'Hector's just got off the train,' said Lachlan. 'They kept him in Arbroath Police Station for an awful long time.'

'Aye,' said Hector, 'and I wasn't happy when Lachlan picked me up and told me he was taking me to yet *another* police station!'

'I'll take you to the pub as soon as we're done here,' said Lachlan. 'Now sit down and keep quiet.' He looked at Nancy. 'Did they catch your uncle?'

Nancy nodded.

'When the police came, he was stuck half-way through the broken window of his study,' said Jamie. 'He was in a bit of a mess. His clothes were all ripped, and there was blood everywhere.'

'I don't have any sympathy for him,' said Nancy. 'I hope it hurt.' A thought suddenly came to her. 'Oh, my, I've got to tell my pa! His own brother, a traitor!' She looked down and her hands were shaking. Jamie reached out and took her hands in his own.

'It'll be all right,' he said.

Jean came in with more mugs of cocoa and placed them in front of the soldiers. 'What's the matter, Nancy?' she asked.

'She's just shaken up,' said Jamie. 'It's been a long night. And we've been hanging around this station for hours waiting for who-knows-what. It must be nearly tea-time! We've been here all day, and they won't tell us anything. They haven't let Nancy see her ma and pa.'

'I know,' said Jean. 'They've had a call from Rosyth. They want you to talk to the Navy folks before you talk to anyone else. Defence of the Realm Act, 1914. They probably just want to make sure you're not going to talk about this to the newspapers. German spies running around Dundee, plotting the sinking of Royal Navy ships? That's not something we want to spread around.' Nancy looked worried. 'Oh, Nancy, don't look so concerned. You've been so brave up until now.'

'I wasn't being brave,' said Nancy. 'I was just doing my duty. Hector and Lachlan went off to fight. You volunteered to help the police, Jean. Why shouldn't I have done my bit?'

'I don't know why *I* did it,' said Jamie quietly.

'Jamie Balfour, you did your duty the same as me,' said Nancy.

'No,' said Jamie. 'I didn't. I don't believe in all that stuff. I think my pa was crazy to go off to fight. I think the whole war is stupid.'

'Wait a moment,' said Hector. 'Jamie Balfour? Any relation to Duncan Balfour, 4th Battalion of the Black Watch? Dark hair, sharp nose, could sing like an angel?'

Jamie started in surprise. 'That's my pa,' he said.

'Doesn't surprise me,' said Hector. 'You're as brave as your father was, lad. I lost this eye at Neuve-Chapelle, but I'd have lost a lot more if your father hadn't been there. Some people do their duty for King and Country,' he nodded at Nancy, 'like this brave wee lassie. But others do the right thing for their friends and loved ones. Your father never cared about King or Kaiser, but he knew his mates were going into battle, and he needed to be there to help them.' He looked Jamie right in the eye. 'Just like you did with Nancy.'

Jamie didn't know what to say. Fortunately, at that moment the desk sergeant appeared at the door again.

'The Navy bloke is here,' he said, and waved through a young man, not much older than Jamie and Nancy.

'Good afternoon,' said the officer. 'I'm Midshipman Melville, and we need to talk about spies.'

EPILOGUE

HMS *ARGYLL* was deemed to be beyond repair, so the Navy salvaged what they could, including her guns, then demolished her, sending the wreck to the bottom of the North Sea, where it remains to this day.

THE CREW OF THE *ARGYLL* was rescued by HMS *Jackal* and HMS *Hornet* without a single loss or injury, save for one sprained ankle.

CAPTAIN JAMES TANCRED faced a court-martial, but remained in the Royal Navy and rose to the rank of Vice-Admiral. However, after losing the *Argyll*, he never commanded another ship.

MIDSHIPMAN HARRY MELVILLE had an illustrious career in the Royal Navy, the details of which have not been made available to the public.

ADMIRAL SIR JOHN JELLICOE led the Royal Navy Grand Fleet at the Battle of Jutland in May 1916, which remains the world's largest clash of dreadnoughts.

COMMANDER THE HONOURABLE EDWARD

BINGHAM, the captain of HMS *Hornet*, whose manoeuvring skill effected the rescue of most of the *Argyll's* crew, continued to serve with distinction and earned the Victoria Cross for his bravery in leading a destroyer division into battle against the enemy fleet. After the war, he remained with the Royal Navy, and retired as a Rear Admiral in 1932.

THE BELL ROCK LIGHTHOUSE was automated in 1988, and continues to provide a beacon in the North Sea for all shipping. The masonry on which the lighthouse rests has been battered by the sea for over two hundred years without being replaced or adapted, but remains solid, a testament to the skill of the engineers who built it.

ASSISTANT KEEPER COLIN McCORMACK took to his bed for the rest of the day to settle his nerves and recover from his rope burns.

JEAN THOMSON was appointed as a 'police sister' after the war ended in 1918, which involved patrolling, interviewing, and escorting women and girls, effectively making her Scotland's first policewoman. There is a memorial plaque to this remarkable woman at the Marketgait entrance to the Tayside Police Headquarters.

HECTOR MUNRO and LACHLAN FRASER completed their convalescence and returned to their village on the Dornoch Firth, the only members of their 'pals battalion' who made it through the war. They set up a ship's chandler business together, and remained friends for the rest of their lives.

STUART CAIRD (Uncle Stuart) was taken to the Tower of London and interrogated by British Military Intelligence. It is assumed that he was executed by firing squad, but no record of the execution has been found.

JAMIE BALFOUR and NANCY CAIRD remained friends, kept getting into trouble, continued to stick their noses in where they weren't wanted, and solved more crimes in and around Dundee than the City of Dundee Police. Jamie went back to live with his mother, and if it wasn't always easy living there, he was at least assured of a second home at the Caird house whenever he needed it. The stories of their later adventures are yet to be told.

ACKNOWLEDGEMENTS

Writing this book would not have been possible without the information provided by William Daysh, MBE, RN (Retd) in his essay, 'The death of HMS *ARGYLL*', available on the bellrock.org.uk website. I have taken enormous liberties with the story, including the invention of a German spy plot, a secret dossier, and the details of all the conversations, but I have tried to keep to the chronology of the events laid down by Mr. Daysh from the point of view of the sailors on board the *Argyll*.

The diaries of Midshipman Norman Calder, an Australian in the Royal Australian Navy who was posted to a Royal Navy ship, *HMS Sovereign*, at Scapa Flow during the First World War, are available at *www. pbenyon.plus.com/Scapa_Diary/Index.html*—this account of a young man, not much more than a boy, and his life in the Navy make fascinating reading. It's somewhat disconcerting when he describes having his first shave in October 1917—midshipmen in those days were little more than boys, which gives you a real appreciation for their bravery.

Details of lighthouse life are mostly remembered stories from my dad Robert, who was a lightkeeper for the Northern Lighthouse Board for twenty years. Although, in my dad's stories, there was a lot more swearing and flatulence and mickey-taking than I've included in this current book.

Thanks must go to Colin Jones, who provided encouragement, camaraderie, and a long list of typos from the first draft.

Thank you to everyone involved in the Great War Dundee Children's Book Prize. I'm immensely grateful to everyone at Dundee Libraries and Schools who organised the competition, especially Fiona, Elaine, Moira and Judy. Thanks to the judges Theresa Breslin, Allan Burnett, and Martha Payne. And an especially big thank you to all the schoolchildren from Dundee who were involved in the competition, reading the books, voting on them, designing covers for the shortlisted books, and doing an amazing job at the prize ceremony. I've been overwhelmed by the enthusiasm they've shown for the competition. Special mention must go to Qynn Herd, who came up with the design that formed the basis of the cover art.

Thanks to Kirsten Couper of the Arbroath Signal Tower Museum for her enthusiasm for the book and all things related to the Bell Rock, and for inviting me to visit the scene of Nancy and Jamie's showdown with the spies.

Thanks to everyone at Cargo Publishing for helping make my dream come true, especially Helen Sedgwick for editing this book into something I can be really proud of. Thanks to the folk at Freight Books for fostering the book through its first year, and most of all many thanks to Anne at Cranachan for adopting *The Wreck of the Argyll* and giving it a new home.

Last but not least, I am grateful to my partner Sandra, without whose patience and support I'd never be able to write down all these stories that fill my head.

ABOUT THE AUTHOR

John K Fulton is the son of a lighthouse keeper, and grew up all around the coast of Scotland. These remote and lonely locations instilled in him a life-long love of books and the sea. He studied at the universities of St. Andrews and Dundee, and now lives in Leicester with his partner Sandra. While Leicester is about as far from the sea as you can get in the UK, their home is stuffed with books, which is the next-best thing.

His first book, the WWI spy thriller *The Wreck of the Argyll*, won the Great War Dundee Children's Book Prize. His second book, *The Beast on the Broch*, goes back even further into Scottish history to the time of the Picts and the Vikings.

You can contact John at www.johnkfulton.com, on Twitter @johnkfulton, or as johnkfulton on Instagram.

YOU MIGHT ALSO ENJOY...

The Beast on the Broch
by John K. Fulton
Scotland, 799 AD. Talorca befriends a strange Pictish beast; together, they fight off Viking raiders.

Charlie's Promise
by Annemarie Allan
A frightened refugee arrives in Scotland on the brink of WW2 and needs Charlie's help.

Fir for Luck
by Barbara Henderson
The heart-wrenching tale of a girl's courage to save her village from the Highland Clearances.

A Pattern of Secrets
by Lindsay Littleson
Jim must save his brother from the Poor House in this gripping Victorian mystery.

Punch
by Barbara Henderson
Runaway Phin's journey across Victorian Scotland with an escaped prisoner and a dancing bear.

The Revenge of Tirpitz
by M. L. Sloan
The thrilling WW2 story of a boy's role in the sinking of the warship Tirpitz.

THANK YOU FOR READING

Pokey Hat publishes vibrant, imaginative and entertaining fiction titles, but we also want our readers to escape to Scotland by experiencing something of our exciting culture and history, wherever they live in the world.

We hope you enjoyed reading and sharing *The Wreck of the Argyll*, whether at school, at home, or cooried under the covers, and that it has brought the *story* in hi*story* to life.

Please tell all your friends and tweet us with your *#TheWreckoftheArgyll* feedback, or better still, write an online review to help spread the word!

Find us online at

cranachanpublishing.co.uk

and follow us

@cranachanbooks

for news of our forthcoming titles.

pokey hat